CW01189478

BY THE SAME AUTHOR

Fiction

Waterdrops

The Plotting

Summer Nineteen Forty-Five

The Hotel of Dreams and Other Stories

Julia

Remembered Acts

The Life in Us

Praise for John Lucas

'Lucas's [*Waterdrops*] is a mystery-like series of Russian dolls, an entralling narrative ... Lucas's is a beautiful, profoundly charitable art.'

Paul Binding, *Independent*

'[*Waterdrops*] is a splendid novel. I couldn't put it down.'

Merryn Williams, *Oxford Mail*

'A fine and extraordinary novel [*Waterdrops*]. Sombre, troubled, intricate, deeply searching – philosophical, to some extent perhaps, in the way Greek tragedy is?'

Richard Kell

'Lucas knows how to fill in those little details – a tune title, lines from a poem, the way musicians relate on and off the stand, a literary reference, a specific location – that give [*The Plotting*] credibility.'

Jim Burns, *The Northern Review of Books*

'John Lucas's moving, enthralling *Summer Nineteen Forty-Five* ... '

Books of the Year, *Times Literary Supplement*

'The novel, that bright book of life – as Lawrence would have it – is more than an amusement. It has things to tell us about living, about the true relations of men and women. John Lucas employs a lighter touch than his illustrious predecessor, but in his new novel, *Julia*, he too is concerned with what draws men and women together, and what may sunder them.'

Stuart Henson, *The London Grip*

'A wonderful read. I had to drag myself away from it to finish this review.'
  Tim Thorne, *New Writing* (Australia) on *Remembered Acts*

'*The Life in Us* ... an absorbing, touching novel.'
              Paul McDonald, The London Grip

THAT LITTLE THREAD

THAT LITTLE THREAD

JOHN LUCAS

GREENWICH EXCHANGE
LONDON

ACKNOWLEDGEMENTS

To my publisher, James Hodgson, of Greenwich Exchange: one of the best independent publishing companies. For information about the world of tax advisers, Professor Peter Swann, and Jenny Swann for information about pre-natal matters in 1960s. For her superb copy editing, Rachel Lucas. And as always, to Pauline.

Greenwich Exchange, London

First published in Great Britain in 2023
All rights reserved

John Lucas © 2023

This book is sold subject to the conditions that it shall not, by way of trade or otherwise, be lent, resold, hired out or otherwise circulated without the publisher's prior consent in any form of binding or cover other than that in which it is published and without a similar condition including this condition being imposed on the subsequent purchaser.

Printed and bound by imprintdigital.com
Cover design: December Publications
Tel: 07951511275

Greenwich Exchange Website: www.greenex.co.uk

Cataloguing in Publication Data
is available from the British Library

ISBN: 978-1-910996-67-6

for my family

> 'simply the thing I am
> Shall make me live'
> – Parolles, *All's Well That Ends Well*

> 'ALONE: quite by oneself, unaccompanied,
> without other companion.'
> – *Oxford English Dictionary*

> What is there
>
> like fortitude! What sap
>   went through that little thread
>   to make the cherry red!
> – Marianne Moore

1

AT TEN MINUTES PAST FIVE, PETER Simpson left his room, closing the door firmly behind him, pushed through the heavy glass swing doors at the end of the ground floor corridor, and exited the Arts building.

In warm, early autumn sunshine he strolled toward the faculty car park, passing en route a sprinkling of students, some of whom he knew and greeted with a smile and a raised hand and, as he reached his car, transferred his briefcase from right to left hand before reaching into his trouser pocket in order to retrieve his car key.

As he did so, he became aware from the reflection in the driver's window that a man was standing behind him. Alarm prickled. Recently there had been a spate of on-campus car thefts, muggings too, some carried out in daylight. The car park, part-surrounded by high hedges, was some distance from the nearest building, and Peter guessed he was out of earshot of the students he'd encountered on his way here.

He turned. 'Can I help you?'

But this man surely couldn't be a danger. He was dressed in a grey business suit, expensively-tailored, white shirt set off by a neat, sage-green tie, and his dark-brown suede shoes were, Peter could see at a glance, unscuffed. Recognition flickered.

'Peter Simpson? *Professor* Simpson?' The ironic inflection in the way the man pronounced Peter's newly acquired title was unmissable, and it was accompanied by a slight twitch of the lips. 'Don't you know me? Have I changed so much?'

The voice was the same. Peter allowed himself the briefest of nods.

'You've changed,' he said. 'At least you've changed the way you dress.'

'You haven't,' the other man said. 'Open-neck shirt, jacket from Marks and Sparks, Mr Academic Everyman.' The smile barely hid his – derision, was it? From his breast pocket, he withdrew a black leather wallet and from it chose a business card, which he handed to Peter without bothering to speak.

The card said T.W. DEVINE: TAX ADVISER, and below was a telephone number and what Peter knew to be an office address, somewhere in London.

He pushed the card into his breast pocket. 'I don't suppose I'll ever be in need of a tax adviser,' he said. 'Still, if I do I'll know who to consult.' And when the other kept silent, he added, 'Long time no see.' He extended his right hand. 'You remembered where I worked then. Still work.'

'Work is it? I thought you liked to say that being a university lecturer was "a privilege, not like work at all." The cat that got the cream. That's what I was told, anyway.' A smile flickered on and quickly off.

Before Peter could answer, a colleague of his, Simon Tims, came calling out as he lumbered across the car park toward where the two of them stood.

'Peter, a word. Have you heard that old Buggerlugs wants to hold a staff meeting next Wednesday? Why? We had one at the beginning of term, and *this* time he wants to hold it in the afternoon, if you please.'

Peter nodded. 'I know,' he said.

'Well, can't you get him to change it? At least to the morning.'

'He works in the morning,' Peter said, 'we all do. It's when we're chained to our desks, deep in research.'

'Very bloody funny,' Simon said. 'I'm supposed to be playing football that afternoon. A key game against Clifton Staff. I can't afford to miss it, and my old gran's already died twice this year. I daren't risk bumping her off for a third time.'

He turned to look at Peter's companion. 'Sorry for interrupting your confab,' he said, 'but this is important.'

'Sounds like it,' DeVine said, but Tims' attention was fixed on Peter. He shook his brush of greying hair in exasperation as he pleaded with him to 'speak to the Big White Chief, can't you, you've got the pull, Professor, at least get him to change the time of the meeting,' before nodding to DeVine. 'Nice meeting you,' he said, and strode heavily away.

'Who's he when he's at home?' DeVine asked. When Peter gave the name, adding, 'Lecturer in Chaucerian Studies,' DeVine said, 'and new since Paddy's time, I'm guessing. I don't remember her ever mentioning that name.'

'No,' Peter said, 'she wouldn't have known him. Simon's a recent arrival.'

But DeVine was no longer interested. 'In answer to your question,' he said, 'I didn't have to make much of an effort to discover you were still here. As you may have noticed, I don't visit these parts any longer, but I was passing through so I thought I'd drop in, look you up, see how you were getting on. A phone call to University Enquiries was all it took. And no, I didn't need to speak with Professor Simpson, as you've now become. Congratulations on that, by the way. But no, no need to say who was asking after him.'

He paused. 'And now you're going to ask me why I wanted

– want – to make contact. Given that the two of us only met once or twice, and that was ... was before.'

He was looking closely at Peter now, who, without speaking, stared evenly back at him. 'Well, this is the truth. I'm here because I'm hoping you can help me. Cards on the table, straight up, I need to talk.'

Peter was genuinely mystified. 'Talk? Talk about what?'

From time to time former students would contact him out of the wish to renew acquaintance. There were others with whom he'd remained friends over the years and one or two wrote to him because they were wondering about the advisability of part-time research. What did he think of their proposed subject? And might he agree to supervise them? He was invariably pleased to hear from them, happy to know that their undergraduate years had been enjoyable, even life-changing, and that in employment, ostensibly remote from their academic studies, they remained grateful to their tutors.

But this was different. Terry DeVine hadn't been a student of his, hadn't had any connection with the university bar the one, and Peter had little reason to feel anything other than a kind of fading, perhaps irrational anger mixed with a lasting sadness. Was this why he was facing someone who to all appearances was a successful businessman, now in his early middle age and very different from the pushy, at best louche hang-about, who'd briefly crossed his path twenty years earlier.

'I can't talk for long,' he said. 'I'm on chef's duty for this evening and I mustn't be late home.'

Stop. That's enough. He remembered an Australian friend of his whose advice was always, 'Say what you've got to say and then shut up.' He had no desire to talk to this man. Nothing to hide, but nothing either to say.

'This won't take long, I promise,' DeVine's smile was meant to be reassuring. 'But I'd rather not talk here, in the open. I've left my car at The Swan. If you can give me a lift that far

I'll buy you a drink and you'll be on your way inside half-an-hour. That OK?'

It wasn't really a question, Peter sensed, and as he did so, felt he should resent the fact that DeVine was as good as taking control. *Do as I say, chop, chop.* The business man's way, presumably.

'Alright,' he said, 'but half-an-hour is as much as I can spare.'

He unlocked his car and as DeVine walked round to the passenger seat, Peter reached across and pushed the door open for him.

'Here we go,' he said, turning the key in the ignition before he could stop himself repeating the words he'd habitually spoken – chanted rather – with the young Paul and Sally strapped into the back seat, setting off on a family holiday.

But DeVine gave no sign of having heard.

A few minutes later, Peter pulled into the car park of The Swan, and as they climbed from the battered VW, DeVine, without bothering to thank him for the lift, led the way into the pub's saloon bar.

2

ALTHOUGH IT WAS STILL SOME MINUTES short of six o'clock, The Swan was beginning to fill with early-evening drinkers, most of them students, one or two of whom Peter recognised and acknowledged with a nod and brief smile.

The pair of them chose a table toward the rear of the saloon bar, and as they settled into their chairs Peter said, 'Before we go any further, tell me how you came to be waiting by my car.'

'I wasn't waiting,' DeVine said. 'I followed you when you left the building. I'd wanted to see if you were in your room, to which some polite young Miss had directed me, but I was too late, and then you stopped to speak to someone – a student? – so I hung back until you were on your own.'

He looked around him and said, 'This boozer's a bit different from how it used to be. Furniture, light fittings, carpet ... and a new landlord, too. I guess old Grayson left the scene some years ago?'

Peter nodded as he raised his glass. 'And many years should see some change,' he said. In answer to the other man's questioning look, he said 'Dylan Thomas.'

DeVine, raising his own glass, said, 'Once an academic ... '
'You'd not find many quoting Thomas these days,' Peter said. He drank some beer. 'Now,' he added as he glanced at his watch, 'I'd like you to tell me why you're here, and why you want to talk to me.'

DeVine swallowed most of his pint, slowly brushed the back of his fingers across his lips, lowered his glass to the table, then, directing his glance away, said, 'Depends how much you remember about that time.'

There was a pause. And now he was looking directly at Peter.

'I remember that you went off with one of the best students I ever taught,' Peter said. 'At Easter. Before she'd had a chance to sit her exams and get the First that was hers for the taking.'

'And you don't know why?'

Peter hesitated for a moment, then said, evasively, 'I never heard from her again.' As DeVine went on staring at him, he said, 'I know she wrote to our secretary, saying that she was resigning from the course but was hoping to take it up again later, though that didn't explain anything. And she apparently gave her parents' address in Hamburg, in case the University wanted to contact her. That apart, nothing.'

He knew, but he wanted to hear the story from DeVine's own lips.

'But you wrote to her.'

Again, Peter took his time before replying, this time diverted by the antics of a group of students at the bar who were encouraging one of their number, a young woman, to swallow a glass of beer without drawing breath. She was bent double, spluttering, and to ironic cheers she gave up the attempt, handing the glass to the person nearest her before she half-staggered, half-ran to the toilets. Some things never changed.

He turned back to DeVine. 'Yes, I wrote to her. I told her

I was sorry she'd not stayed to complete her degree but that if she ever wanted to return and finish her course she'd have my full support. I think I added words to the effect that I was sure she had it in her to do well.'

'But she never replied?'

'No, because I'd sent it to her hall of residence address and by the time it was forwarded to her in Germany she was already dead.'

'Ah, so you know that.'

'Yes, I know that. And I know that she died in childbirth. And if you're interested as to *how* I know that, as you probably are, it's because her father wrote to the Vice-Chancellor. I never saw the letter but I was told the details, his fury that the University had failed in its duty of acting "in loco parentis", his determination to bring that failure to the attention of as many responsible people as possible, to "drag the University's reputation through the mud, where it belongs", I think were his words.'

DeVine's eyes locked onto Peter's as he asked, 'And did he?'

'He may have written to some newspapers, contacted an MP or two, but if so nothing much came of it. I imagine the University solicitors knew how to handle him. Anyway, this was the late 60s, and women the age of eighteen and older were supposed to take responsibility for their own lives.'

Peter paused, looked away, then back at DeVine. 'I assume you were the father.'

It wasn't a question, and when DeVine nodded, Peter said, 'Of course.' He drank some more of his beer and said, 'From time to time I'd see you together in this place, and once, I seem to remember, she introduced you to me and you offered to buy me a drink.'

'And you turned me down. Never accept a drink from a stranger, especially not a bit of rough.' The hint of a sneer in DeVine's words grated.

'I was worried for her. I was certain she had a bright future ahead of her.'

'She should have been alone in her room studying, not spending her evenings with some Flash Harry?'

'That's about the measure of it,' Peter said.

A further pause, anger momentarily subdued by curiosity, before he said, 'Not that it's any business of mine, but what brought you together?'

'Perhaps she preferred me to all the chinless wonders who hovered round her whenever she came to The Swan with a friend or two. Flies to the honey pot. All those Hoorah Henries and Bollox Berties.'

The words came from a mouth taut with contempt. DeVine cleared his throat. 'So how did boy meet girl? She was in here one night, standing at the bar with a girlfriend, reached for her drink, knocked it over, I offered to buy a replacement. And that, minus several chapters, is the story of how town and gown got together.'

'Well, congratulations,' Peter said, and at once wished he'd not done so.

The young woman who a few moments earlier had fled the scene now rejoined her companions at the bar, white-faced but determined to pass off what had happened as a joke. She was laughing, gesticulating, and to applause and cheers Peter heard her say, 'There must have been beer in the something.'

'Don't be so fucking condescending.' DeVine's anger was genuine, urgent. He paused, controlling his voice before he next spoke. 'For your information, Paddy was my love,' he said, speaking slowly. 'The woman I adored.'

Peter was shaken by the intensity with which the words were uttered, 'That was thoughtless of me,' he said. 'I'm sorry.' His smile meant as rueful appeasement, he watched DeVine unclenching his fists, waited as the man's shoulders relaxed, and then said, 'You call her Paddy, but I knew her as Beatrice.

Beatrice Connor. That was the name she put at the head of her essays and exam papers. Beatrice, Dante's muse, his inspiration. It seemed a good name for your ... for someone so brilliant and – and attractive.'

The other man sat for a moment in silence, head bowed, and when he roused himself to look at Peter, Peter saw that his eyes were glazed by tears. DeVine flicked them away, and said simply, 'Paddy was her chosen nickname, the name she liked friends to use, the name *I* always called her. Always. Never Beatrice, never. That was the name her parents christened her with, the name of some long-dead aunt who'd had royal blood in her, so they told her. She hated it, hated most things to do with her parents, her father especially.' He laughed mirthlessly. 'She had it in for him alright. "Mr Falutin Faultless", she called him.'

Peter thought for a moment but said anyway, 'So she went for you as the polar opposite. The street boy with the heart of gold.' Because it came to him that for all DeVine's classy suit, the Jaguar he'd pointed out as Peter brought his VW to a halt in The Swan's car park, the real DeVine was no more and no less than a street boy made good. Arthur Seaton, Billy Straight-Talker.

DeVine stared at him, the glimmer of a smile on those taut lips. 'Yes,' he said, 'got me bang to rights, Mr Lecturer. I was a street boy, good as, anyway. Though my street was Orphanage Row. A bit of a bastard, a foundling, that's me. And Paddy and me, we met by chance in this pub. Heiress meets Scruff. Fate brought us together care of a spilt drink. Corny or what.'

He drank the rest of his beer, stood, and when Peter, shaking his head, put a hand over his own half-full glass, DeVine went to the bar and almost immediately returned with a whisky. 'The other half,' he said.

Sitting, he raised the glass, drank most of the whisky in one swallow, and said, 'And now I guess you want to know what I was doing in your city in the first place.'

'Being a travelling salesman,' Peter said.

DeVine silently applauded. 'Got it in one. I was having a drink after concluding a successful bit of business. October, it was, when a publican's thoughts begin to turn to the Festive Season. The Swan, like other hostelries, was already planning its Christmas jollies, getting fags and booze in early to avoid disappointment, Ho! Ho!' He paused, inspected his glass, and then, more seriously said, 'Paddy had called in for a half of cider with her mate before they went off to the flicks. I can even remember the title of the film, *Two for the Road*, Albert Finney and Audrey Hepburn, how about that – and, no, I didn't buy her a further drink, not that night, anyway. But next week, it was different. This time she was on her own, careful not to look in my direction when she came up to the bar, where I stood, all careless indifference. But when I touched her elbow she swung round and, blushing I'd swear, was keen for me to know she'd dropped in because she wanted to return the favour. Hoped I might be there – blush, blush – had seen me on a few previous occasions, so knew I used the place on a regular basis ... '

As DeVine talked on, for the first time Peter began to sense the allure of the other man's physical presence, his almost magnetic pull, he could imagine DeVine's appeal for a young, and, at a guess, relatively innocent woman. What he couldn't imagine was the attraction that Beatrice – Paddy – held for Terry DeVine. Or was it her very innocence that drew him to her, combined with a springy energy which, twenty years ago, had pulsed through her and seemingly lit all her movements, her talk, her looks.

And now DeVine was speaking again, this time as if he had a need to communicate with someone – anyone – willing to hear him out.

'A few months, that's all we had,' he said. 'Her and me. I'd come up from London every weekend, we'd go to a hotel, and then on Sunday evenings she'd say goodbye, get back to hall to prepare for Monday classes and I'd be out on the road, flogging goods.'

He paused, shook his head. 'And then, in early March, things got a bit sticky. Paddy found out she was pregnant, three months gone. OK by me. In fact, more than OK. I was on Cloud Number Seven. I'd got enough to put down money on a flat, though we agreed to keep everything on hold until she'd taken her exams. After that, we'd marry, sure enough, but before then we'd keep it to ourselves. Classes would soon be coming to an end, and after Easter there'd be no need to stick around all that much. She'd tell a few close friends, but nobody else need know. "Suits me," I told her, though I was happy as Larry, I can tell you. Dreams of having my own family. But there was an exception to all this keeping the news to ourselves. She'd have to tell her parents about me, about us, about her being pregnant, and about our plans to get married in the summer, soon as she'd got her degree.'

'Which presumably thrilled them no end.'

DeVine's smile was more by way of a grimace. His gaze was turned inward as though he'd forgotten Peter, possessed by his memories.

'She wrote them a letter. Big mistake, that. Next thing her father tells her he'll be flying over, wants to meet me. Wanted no doubt to buy me off. A business man with a top job in Germany, he must have been worth a pile. A man with a reputation to take care of, that was how he'd have seen it. He'd probably got some bloke or other earmarked to become part of the family jewels.'

'So what happened?'

DeVine was jerked back to awareness of Peter's presence. 'Paddy told him I was unavoidably out of the country. Har, har. I think she was worried that if we met it might come to blows. Her father was a bully, as big as a bear and with a bear's temper. She'd told me about him, about how the world had to run according to his timetable. Anyone standing in his way better step to one side. From all Paddy let drop, I got the impression his wife had to jump whenever he said jump, though she'd learnt to copy some of his airs and graces.'

'The two of you didn't meet, I take it.'

'Not then, no. He flew back to Hamburg after telling Paddy her parents didn't approve of all this hole-and-corner behaviour, and we thought we'd seen the last of him, that he was off our backs.' A shake of the head. 'No chance of that. A month later he was on the blower, May, that was. Told Paddy that her mother was seriously ill, needed to see her pronto. Perhaps she *was* ill, her mother, living with that bastard.'

DeVine stared into his glass. 'Paddy had told me plenty about their happy family life. About how he decided everything for the three of them: where they holidayed, what clothes they wore, where Paddy went to school – private, of course – and which school friends were suitable for the daughter of a top businessman.'

'In Hamburg?'

'No, London. The move to Hamburg only happened once Paddy was leaving to go to university. Some Mr Top-Table-Biggest came knocking on his door, offered him a once-in-a-lifetime chance to make a fortune. Before then it was Highgate.'

Peter nodded. 'I see.' Then, glancing at his watch, he said, 'I'm sorry, but I really must get to my domestic duties.'

He paused and said by way of an apologetic smile, in an attempt to explain his desire to get away, 'Is there much more you want to tell me? I assume that Beatrice – Paddy – did go to see her mother? It must have been around Easter time when her father made contact, term over, no reason she couldn't go. Besides, her mother ... '

DeVine nodded, but said nothing, and into the silence, Peter spoke again. 'By the way,' he said, as he made to stand, 'those last weeks of term, I was beginning to wonder about Paddy, I admit. At first I put it down to nerves. Finals approaching, and she knew how much I, and others who'd taught her, were expecting her to do well. On one or two occasions – no more – she seemed distracted in class, and I couldn't help noticing that in spite of the weather, one of the warmest Aprils in years, she always came dressed in a coat she never removed. I even wondered whether I should ask her if anything was wrong. But I couldn't think what to say. A tutor has to step carefully. You can invite confidences but you certainly can't demand any. I'd noticed that you and she weren't to be found any longer in The Swan. Had you perhaps broken up? Had you, yourself, cleared off? It was a possibility, but of course I couldn't ask her about it.'

He stopped, affected by DeVine's suddenly evident distress, the way he winced and then ducked his head. Then he said, 'Or are you about to tell me that she – that Paddy – was tricked into going to Hamburg so her father could, well, abduct her? She was twenty-one at least, wasn't she? He wouldn't be allowed to get away with it.'

DeVine shook his head. 'It wasn't that,' he said, turning to watch as the group at the bar made a noisy exit into the dusk.

When he looked back his eyes were again cloudy with tears which this time he made no attempt to blink away. The last pretence of stoical resolution had disappeared. 'Of course, we had our suspicions, so I agreed to go with her. Difficult, though. I couldn't afford to be away from work for more than a couple of days over a weekend. By then – this was early June – I'd got a new job, working for an accountancy firm – better pay, better prospects, take some exams, learn the ins and outs as you go – but I needed to be at my desk, Monday to Friday, nine to five. If what we found at Hamburg was kosher, then Paddy would stay on for a few days.'

He exhaled heavily. 'That was when she decided to give

up on her degree course. It was all too much for her, poor love. I tried to get her to change her mind, pointed out to her that classes had come to an end now Spring Term was over, but she wasn't having it. She was in no state of mind to sit exams, couldn't begin to do herself justice.'

A sad shake of the head. 'I couldn't argue with that. Soooo.' The word came out as a prolonged sigh. 'Off we went to Hamburg early one Saturday morning, found a small hotel, and she took a taxi on her own to see her mother.'

Another pause. 'She phoned late that evening. Her mother was clearly ill and Paddy had decided to stay overnight to be at her side. She'd join me for breakfast. But early next morning *another* phone call. Plans altered. She wanted to be with her mother for a few more hours, but she'd do her best to be back with me by lunchtime and we'd go out to eat somewhere nice before getting the train to London. "Kisses, hugs, be careful not to look at Hamburg women."'

'"As if," I said, and asked whether I should come to collect her, but she was determined not to let her father clap eyes on me. So I checked out of our room, the room she'd never even spent the night in, sat over coffee in the hotel bar, and waited. And waited. She eventually arrived looking tired out. She'd been up most of the night coping with her mother's sickness, and now that she – the mother – had been taken to hospital, felt too tired herself to travel back to London, not in her condition. I'd have to return on my own, and as soon as she possibly could she'd rejoin me. I reminded her I'd found a flat for us, and we were due to move in at the beginning of July. Wellingborough, halfway between London and the University and, of course, I was still hoping she'd change her mind, call back the letter she'd written to you and take her exams, get her degree.'

DeVine tipped back his glass, drained the contents. 'By late afternoon I was back in London.' He was hurrying his narration up as Peter buttoned his jacket, shifted from one foot to the other. 'Don't go yet,' he said. 'Please. I haven't finished.' And when Peter said, 'Two more minutes, then I *must* go,' DeVine, leaning across the table to grip Peter's wrist, said, 'Listen to this, will you. That evening I got another call, this time from London. Her mother's sister. "Beatrice is in hospital. There are complications. I am instructed to tell you not to try to get in touch."'

Peter watched attentively, as DeVine said, 'What complications? She wasn't much more than seven months gone and she was in good health, *and* she was having regular check-ups from her doctor. Anyway, she wasn't due till later in the year.' He stared at Peter. 'As for "*Instructed.*" No prizes for guessing who'd told her to say that.'

He picked up his glass and, seeing it was empty, returned it to the table. 'Well, bugger him. I was all set to fly straight over to Hamburg, to see her, my love, but when I phoned their house to tell them I was on my way and sod them if they didn't like it, it was the mother who answered. She was in tears, yelling at me. I don't remember the exact words, couldn't really understand what she was trying to tell me. She was crying, almost hysterical. But then I got the message. Her daughter, my Paddy, was dead.'

Again he picked up the glass, turned it upside down, righted it, and, when he could manage to control his voice, his hands suddenly shaking, said, 'So now you know.' There was a long pause, before he said, 'Of course, it was *his* doing, that was what I reckoned. Should I fly over? But what would be the point? I needed to clear my head, but all I could think was that it was, it *had* to be his fault. Chances were she'd said something to offend the pompous bastard, he'd lost his temper, struck her, knocked her down, and in her condition that was it. Her father had killed her, killed the woman I loved.'

Head down, he repeated the words, whispered them to

himself: 'Paddy, my love.' It sounded theatrical but Peter knew it wasn't.

For some moments he could think of nothing to say. He began to reach out his hand toward DeVine's bowed head but withdrew it without touching the man. DeVine's distress was an unreachable misery. He glanced momentarily around the bar, took in the inconsequential sounds of people talking and laughing together, the everyday casualness of social circumstance, the to-fro traffic of words and gestures that belonged in a world that knew nothing – how could it – of the sadness, the grief, in the room.

After the silence between them had lasted several minutes, Peter finally extended his hand, let it lie on DeVine's arm and then moved it gently back and forth. And as DeVine looked up, he said, tentatively, wondering at his own voice, 'Do you mind me asking about the ... the baby? I suppose it died too?'

To his surprise and relief, DeVine, having lifted his head and stared at Peter as though he didn't understand the question and barely recognised the questioner, eventually opened his mouth. 'No,' he said. 'She was OK. She survived.' Then he lapsed back into silence.

Peter picked up his glass, toyed with it, unsure whether to ask further questions. But suddenly DeVine was speaking again, this time letting the words run free of his lips, obviously wanting to tell the full story. 'The baby was fine,' he said. 'They took her back to the Hamburg flat, installed a nurse, made sure she was OK, and then, soon as they could they got her back to England, back to Highgate. After all the legal stuff had been gone through, that was, and *that* didn't take long. Post-mortem, hospital reports, police statement ... no suspicious circumstances, no expert witnesses required other than those called to give evidence. I don't know it all, but he'd have retained a top lawyer.' A pause, then he said, 'I tell you, if I'd been called to give evidence, given my chance, I'd have given them something to think about. But no such luck. I was in England, no legal rights, nothing to require my presence. So, Farewell My Lovely.'

The shrug that accompanied the words was, Peter sensed, a way of indicating DeVine's sense of how easily the world at large could accept the disappearance of the woman who'd been his one true love. And as though to confirm this terrible disjunction, a chorus of guffaws and shouts came from a group of young men at the bar who had their filled glasses raised high as they toasted someone or thing, a birthday perhaps. Rugger buggers, no doubt.

DeVine looked in their direction, contemptuous, then, to Peter, he said, 'See, the parents hadn't sold their London house, and for all I know they chose to come back, leave Hamburg, because they – *he* – felt guilt about their daughter's death. Difficult to credit, but I can't think of any other explanation.'

'You know a good deal,' Peter said, 'if you don't mind my saying so.'

'You mean you'd have thought I'd want to forget all about it, soon enough.'

'Of course, I didn't mean that,' Peter said, contrite because, yes, he had at some level considered the possibility. 'But from what you've said about them – about Paddy's parents – I'd assumed they cut you off as soon as their daughter was in the ground. They'd not let you know what they had in mind, what their plans were. They'd keep you in the dark.'

'*He* did,' DeVine said. 'Didn't even want me to know about the funeral arrangements. But *she* kept in touch. By phone. She let me know that Paddy had been cremated and they'd brought her ashes back to England with them.'

A pause. 'To be honest, she turned out to be not too bad,' he said. 'Guilt, maybe, or, who knows, under all that lacquer she had a beating heart, and saw I was a human being.'

And when Peter looked at him, puzzled, sceptical, he said,

'We got to meet on a few occasions when they were back in Highgate, in their old house, as she told me it was. "We rented it out while we were overseas but we're happy to be home."'

He matched Peter's gaze. 'Get that, "overseas". Hamburg wasn't exotic enough, not for them.'

He checked himself. 'Still, as I say, she wasn't all bad. There were times when old Goldenballs would be away for the night "on business" and, now that I was making a bit of money and, with a two-roomer in Bermondsey, she'd let me go on a visit to Highgate, see my daughter, my little girl. Took all day getting there and back, but it was worth it. That was when she was still a tot, of course, didn't know me from Eve. Once she began to grow I wasn't allowed near the place, though from time to time I'd get phone reports on Pat's progress, as she called her.'

'Short for Patricia?'

'Of course.'

'But why weren't you able – allowed – to see her? You were her father, for god's sake.'

'A father with no rights. Paddy and me weren't married, and I wasn't the sort to have any say in their granddaughter's upbringing.' DeVine's laugh was a huff of contempt. 'Better to let the girl think she'd been delivered by stork. If I'd tried to press for rights of access or whatever the bloody thing's called you can imagine that bastard calling out the cavalry. Hire the best lawyers in the land, cost me money I didn't have trying to take him on, and all for nothing. A mate of mine, one who knew his way around in legal matters, told me I'd not stand a hope in hell. Paddy's mother let me know that her husband had made my daughter a ward of court, so keep your filthy hands off her, if you know what's good for you.

'And that was that. I never saw the girl again, though her grandmother was good enough to tell me that Pat always received the cards and presents I sent for her birthdays and at Christmas. Oh, yeh. More likely they went straight into the rubbish bin. Anyway, I never got a dickie bird by way of a reply, even though I'd put my address in with each of my carefully wrapped presents, even took to sending Pat business cards once I'd got some printed. Signed on the back, *your loving father.* I thought she'd like to know her father wasn't some penniless layabout. But nothing. All I knew was what Paddy's mother cared to tell me, including the news that Pat would be going to the same school as her mother. Of course, she would, of course!'

The raucous cries from the group of rugger players were growing louder by the minute, and Peter realised that both he and DeVine were having to raise their voices in order to be heard above the hubbub.

He looked at his watch. He was now very definitely late. He needed to be at home.

'Let's get out of here,' he said, shouted rather. But then, as he led the way, he suddenly remembered. He reached The Swan's outer door and as DeVine followed him out into the deepening twilight, he said, urgently, half-turning toward the other man, 'You haven't yet told me how you want me to help you.'

And so, leaning against Peter's car while Peter stood waiting, car keys in hand, DeVine told him.

3

PETER WAS IN THE KITCHEN, FRYING chopped onion and mushrooms, when he heard Susan's key in the front door.

'In here,' he called, and a moment later she put her head round the door, said, 'Mmm, smells good. Give me five minutes to shower, make myself respectable,' and had vanished by the time he said, 'We'll be eating pasta. OK?'

'OK,' she called from the stairs, and twenty minutes later they sat down to eat at the kitchen table.

He watched, amused, rapt, as he always was by the grace of her movements. She had pulled the salad bowl to her, unloaded lettuce, fennel, slivers of cucumber onto her side plate, and was now using her fork to turn twists of pasta this way and that before taking a first mouthful.

He said, 'I don't know how you manage it.'

She chewed, swallowed, and then, raising her fork in appreciation of his cooking, asked, 'Manage what?'

'To look so beautiful. A hard day at the chalk face, then two hours rehearsals, then home for a quick shower, climb into sweater and jeans, join the old man for a run-of-the-mill supper, and still ... ' He waved a hand to show silence was more eloquent than speech.

Susan used a finger to flick away a damp tendril of hair from her cheek, sipped from her glass of white wine, and said, 'It's the claret what does it.'

'And we're drinking pinot grigio.'

'Why, so we are,' Susan said. Her dark, wide-eyed pretence of amazement was both comic and as heart stopping as it had been the first time they'd met, some thirty years ago. 'So how was your day, my ravishing little beauty?'

'You go first,' Peter said, 'while I sit here and ogle you.'

'My day? My day was, I think we can agree, nothing out of the usual.' Susan rested the fingers of her right hand – those so-shapely fingers – on her cheek. 'French and Music in the morning with third year groups, and in the afternoon, by way of contrast, Music and French. And then, of course, once classes were dismissed, we had two hours of rehearsal for the autumn concert. Ploughing through Debussy Preludes and choral interlude Number One, Nymphs and Shepherds, would you believe – requested, i.e. ordered – by our new Head of School, and Pritchard he hight; then solo violin with Toby Ellis playing Brahms (Brahms lost); and then, what is intended to be the highlight of the evening, that bloody rock group.'

'Well, at least you didn't have to conduct them,' Peter said, pouring more wine.

Susan reached for her glass, changed her mind, and swiftly cleared her plate before saying, 'That, my love, was excellent, as usual. The food, that is.'

Again, she took up her glass, held it aloft in tribute, and said, 'I'd like to say it was entirely reviving, but nothing could fully revive me after being made to listen to The Blowhards, as they call themselves, work their way through two "original compositions", both in the key of G Major, with words by the lead singer which I shall not repeat, largely because I couldn't make them out, though the few I managed to decipher will probably set the audience clamouring to be released from Hall.'

'I don't believe they were that bad.' Peter was laughing. 'Anyway, I'll find out for myself. Do I need a ticket?'

'Available from all good chemists and public toilets,' Susan said, 'but I can probably smuggle you in. Now, tell me about *your* day.'

As he shared the rest of the bottle between them, Peter said, 'Not as enjoyable as yours, at least not the way it ended.'

'Oh.'

He was serious, Susan could sense. She reached across for his hand, squeezed it, and said, 'I'm sorry.'

'Shall I make coffee?'

'No.' She took her hand away, stood. 'I'll do that while you tell me.'

She came to stand beside him, her still trim figure pressed against his shoulder as she bent to kiss the top of his head. He put his arm round her denim-clad hips, said, 'Temptress,' then pushed her gently away. And as she prepared their coffee he began to tell her about his odd, unexpected encounter with DeVine.

When he had gone a little way with his narration, he turned to look at her as she put heaped spoonsful into the cafetière. 'Terry DeVine.' He spelt out the surname. 'Does it ring any bells?'

Susan thought for a moment, shook her head. 'What year are you talking about – I mean when did you first meet him?' And when he told her, she said, 'All those years ago. At that time, if you can remember, Sally was a toddler and Paul had only just been born. You may have told me about him, and about this Beatrice – Paddy – but I had other matters to occupy my attention.'

She brought the cafetière over to the table, took the two cups from the tray, poured for them both, and, as she sat, said, 'Come to think of it, I do vaguely recall your mentioning a student, a woman you thought was outstanding, and who'd suddenly upped sticks and cleared off with a young man.'

'That was her. Beatrice Connor. Paddy to her friends, apparently. From time to time I'd see her with him – with DeVine – in The Swan, and on one occasion she introduced him to me. "Not a student," she told me, "Terry works for a living." And she made it sound like a rap on the knuckles for any man who chose to be a university undergraduate. At first I wondered whether that meant she was turning her back on her studies, but her written work went on as usual, well researched and well written, and in tutorials she had as much to say as ever, all of it worthwhile. So I stopped worrying. Love must be good for her. I was sure she'd get a First and I lived in hope she'd want to go further, take up some research topic or other.'

'Mmm.' Susan sipped her coffee. Holding the cup in both hands, she smiled wryly, said, 'I remember that you were upset by something that happened to her, but I had other concerns to worry about. If I felt anything about the way you went on about her it would have been jealousy, anger too.'

She paused, studied his look of surprise, or was it reproof. 'I may not have mentioned this before, and I thought I'd managed to bury it. But now, suddenly, with your mention of this – this Paddy – it's all come back, the way I felt then.'

Another pause. Her face was suddenly flushed. 'I *was* jealous and I *was* angry. Not all the time, of course not, but we were once equals and in love, and then we weren't – equals, I mean. I became pregnant, twice, we had precious little money, I was hundreds of miles away from family and friends, and as the days went by the contrast between the two of us began to rankle. Young lecturer out most days with his pick of women students, while wifey, never able to get out for a haircut or a chance to buy new clothes, is stuck at home in a Midlands city where she knows hardly anyone, with two small children to attend to, little innocents requiring her attention every minute of the day, so that she's ready to crawl into bed once she's got them down for the night, and then hubby comes waltzing in, expecting his dinner to be ready on the table, picking up toys from the floor, throwing them off *his* chair, *his* desk, and then, then' – a dramatic pause – 'then he wants to tell wifey of his serious concern for some bloody student who's dared to be picked up by a man, an outsider, a travelling salesman or some such, and how worrying that is when she should be studying for exams, and getting a First, and proving how well she's been tutored, and who's a big boy then ... '

She stopped suddenly. 'Sorry,' she said. She took a deep breath. 'I know this must sound a whinge of self-pity. Life's not fair, boo-hoo.' She forced a smile. 'I shouldn't drink more than one glass of wine when I'm tired. Anyway, it was years ago, though you have to accept that what was important to you then wasn't of much interest to me.'

She looked at him, registered his expression, laughed. 'I'll be the doctor,' she said. 'Do you want to tell me where it hurts?'

He said, shifting in his seat as he did so, 'It's a bit late for me to apologise, I suppose.'

There was silence and then, ruefully, he said, 'Well, anyway, that's me told.'

'I could also tell you that I loved you.'

A pause before she added, 'But as I remember, I needed to tell you that Sally had fallen and scraped her knee and Paul wouldn't eat the food I'd spent half the morning preparing for him. And all the time you were bursting to let me know about Milton's use of rhyme in "Lycidas", or how Wordsworth changed the course of English poetry. See, I can remember *that* whereas I bet you can't remember Sally's learning to recite "Hickory, Dickory Dock", so she could repeat it on her third birthday.'

Peter said, 'I remember that I wasn't able to be at that party, was I? Some meeting or other that ran overtime. I remember *that,* remember her not wanting to kiss me when I arrived home late and tried to say how sorry I was, explain why I'd not been able to get back any sooner. I've always remembered *that.*'

Susan said, 'Well, at least that's something.'

She emptied her coffee cup. 'Now,' she said, 'confession time is over.' She stood, went to him, bent and kissed him on top of his head, and said, 'You may now tell me more about what delayed you from your kitchen duties this evening.' She returned to her seat. 'And it had better be good,' she said.

By way of an answer Peter took DeVine's card from his jacket pocket and slowly pushed it across the table. Susan picked it up, looked at the name and the black lettering: TAX ADVISER. 'What *is* a tax adviser?' she asked.

'No idea,' Peter said, 'though I'm willing to bet it's something to do with cheating the law of the land. Sharp suit, fast car, and no doubt Mr DeVine lives in a posh apartment in some equally posh part of London.'

'So what on earth does he want from you?'

'He wants me to keep a look-out for his daughter.'

Susan looked at her husband disbelievingly. 'Pull the other one,' she said.

'I'm telling you the truth,' Peter said. 'Or rather, I'm telling you what he told me. He says that the baby that Paddy gave birth to, the child *he* fathered, is now a student at this university, and he's hoping I'll agree to keep a kind of avuncular eye on her activities, academic and otherwise.'

Susan leant back in her chair. 'But why ask *you*? He can do that himself. Even if he lives in London he can come up to see her, can't he?' She looked enquiringly at him. 'Anyway, what about her grandparents? They brought her up, they can surely be expected to ...'

She stopped as Peter shook his head. 'No, they can't,' he

said. 'According to him, they've gone back to foreign parts. Spain, this time. Where taxes are lower and the weather and food are both better. Once she'd got to the age of sixteen they decided she could manage perfectly well under the eye of her mother's sister in London. And now that she's a university student they reckon they're done with their duty of looking after her, making sure she attains woman's estate without mishap. She's on her own. Mister DeVine thinks there must have been something of a bust up when the girl said she was planning to apply for a place at the university where her mother had once been a student. Not that she – Patricia – would talk about it when she last met DeVine. They had a row, something to do with his agreeing with the aunt and her grandparents that she'd be better to pitch her tent elsewhere, he could fund her if she wanted. She'd never known her mother, he argued, so why the need for this. And if it came to that, he'd never known *his* mother, or his father... He was an orphan and so was she, good as. Free to go anywhere. He admits he got a bit heated, put matters badly. The upshot was that the girl told him she could certainly manage without *him*. She stormed out of the café where they'd met, and he's not seen her since then. She won't answer his letters, doesn't want anything more to do with him.'

'So the poor girl is entirely on her own. What a mess,' Susan said.

'A mess that started all those years ago,' Peter told her, and when Susan looked enquiringly at him, Peter ran through all he had learnt about the mother, Paddy Connor, from DeVine, of their affair, her becoming pregnant, the manner of her death, the survival of her baby, how it was brought up by her mother's parents, their reluctance to let DeVine see his daughter, though once they were back in England he was allowed a very occasional visit to the house in Highgate, and how, over the years, her grandparents explained the nature of his relationship to the little girl, named Patricia,

Pat for short. And the older she got the more care they took to make clear that he had no legal rights over her. Anyway, for years he was on the road. He certainly wasn't in a position to try to make a home for them both. Besides, if he'd ever made a move in that direction, they'd threatened to go to the law, make their granddaughter a ward of court.

'Could they have done that?'

'No idea, but they were in a position to hire the best legal advice. DeVine wouldn't have stood a chance, so I imagine he thought. At all events, the arrangement held through her childhood. They housed and fed her, and he sent her cards on her birthday and at Christmas, all of which he reckons they probably threw away without letting her see them, though as she grew older he was permitted – never encouraged – to make very occasional visits. From time to time they even let him take her out for a few hours, though according to him, whenever the two of them were out of the house, visiting some park or other, or taking a bus or tube to central London, or even a visit to the flicks, a private detective was in tow.'

'How awful,' Susan said. Abruptly, she stood up from the table. 'I need a glass of water,' she said. 'Shall I pour you a whisky?'

Peter shook his head. 'Better not,' he said. 'I've already had beers and half a bottle of wine. Enough for one evening.'

'"Wine after beer I need not fear,"' Susan said, as she fetched the bottle of malt and a whisky glass and put them in front of him. 'In case you change your mind,' she said.

'"But scotch after wine I must decline."'

Susan looked from him to the malt and back again. He watched as she picked the bottles up, that sinuous movement of her hips, and said, 'Cor, Miss, you're a right smasher.'

She looked back at him. 'Behave yourself,' she told him, and winked.

Watching as she resumed her seat, he said, 'I need to tell you the rest of my story, the story DeVine told me.'

He pushed his chair back, crossed his legs, and said, 'According to him there were occasions when they were out on one of their jaunts and his daughter would take the opportunity to ask him about her mother, about Paddy. Did she herself take after Paddy – Beatrice – in any way? "Yes," DeVine told her. "You have her dark, curly hair, her dark eyes, her manner of walking ... " and then he had to stop, it was becoming too much for him. His own words, those.'

He shook his head, sighed. 'One time his daughter told him that she'd been allowed to see photographs of her mother. They were in an album her grandmother kept locked in a cabinet, and on another occasion, she said, she'd recovered the key her grandmother always dropped into a vase, and, heart in mouth, opened the album, wanting to see for herself. "There was one of you and my mother together," she'd told DeVine, beside a river bank as they sat with their arms round each other. He remembered the occasion, a university rowing match the lovers had gone to soon after they'd met. The photograph had been taken by a friend of Paddy's and he supposed it must have been among the belongings sent on to her parents after her death.

"I expect so," Pat had agreed, though his image was scored through by black ink. "I could just make out your face," she'd told him, "but my grandmother had done her best to – well, make you invisible, destroy you." And she'd added that it was a photograph she'd never been shown, no doubt deliberately.'

Susan shook her head. 'Dreadful,' she said again, speaking as though to herself. 'Trying to make the poor man vanish from existence.'

Peter said, 'When he told me the story I could see he was far more upset by what his daughter had told him than he wanted to admit. As for me, the story reminded me of one of

Hardy's poems, one of his ghost poems, about burning a photograph of a woman in a clearance of old papers and then imagining that as he watched the image of the woman disappear, she herself might somehow have felt she was being made invisible, that the flames had put her to death.' And he shuddered.

Susan looked sceptically at her husband. 'But from what you say, DeVine comes across as a decidedly visible presence.'

Peter nodded, silent. Then he said, 'But he lost his love and he can't properly claim his daughter.' He looked at Susan, then away. 'And I happen to know that he's an orphan.'

She stared at him. 'Yes, you mentioned that earlier. How do you know that?'

'Because he told me, not this evening, but years past, when the two of them were together. It was the first time I came on them, quite by chance, in The Swan, sitting at the back of the room, well away from the bar. I'd dropped in for a pint before getting back to campus for an evening class. I'd not have noticed them, and of course I didn't know him from Adam, but he came over, said his girlfriend, his fiancée-to-be, had urged him to buy me a drink, told me it was his birthday, and asked me to join them. I honestly thought there must have been some mistake, but then, when I looked to where he was pointing, I saw that the young woman was in fact my student, Beatrice Connor. So I went across with him to their table, greeted her – she looked pretty awkward – and said I was delighted she was engaged to be married. Which I wasn't, I have to admit, especially as I could see no ring. "Don't worry, Dr Simpson," she said, "It won't be until after I've taken my finals."'

'Married? Did that mean she'd not be wanting to do research? Still, I had to wish them both good luck for the future, even though I didn't much take to him. A bit too keen to impress me, I thought. I suppose that's how salesmen have to behave. You know, at ease with the world. I made to shake his hand. When he took it, "Terry DeVine," he said, "that's me," and then, seeing my look – difficult not to show surprise when a name like that's given to you – "No idea whether it's my real name, but it's what the orphanage called me. Perhaps they thought I'd come from Heaven." And he laughed.'

Peter raised his eyes to meet his wife's. Susan was on the verge of laughter. 'He told you *that?* I'd say that was quite witty.'

'He did. DeVine. He even spelt it for me. Perhaps he thought it improved his credentials. Anyway, what *do* you do with a name like DeVine. I think – no, I'm certain he wanted me to know he'd got nothing to hide, nothing to be ashamed of.'

'Good for him.'

'Yes, good for him, though I didn't really see it that way, not then. But I could tell he was genuinely proud of *and* in love with Paddy. And she was in love with him, alright. You could see it at a glance. No faking there.'

'And how had the lovebirds met. I mean, she was a university student ... '

'And he was a travelling salesman, and good at it, I'd guess. At all events, before I could get away he was keen to let me know that his order book was always full – soft drinks, mostly, but other goodies for pubs, bars, and restaurants. Which is of course how they'd met. In The Swan. Goodies is my word, by the way, he called them "requisites", though with a bit of a wink and a nudge. When we talked today he was keen to remind me how the two of them had got together. According to him he'd been attracted to her from the first time he saw her in The Swan, and one evening, heart in mouth, he got lucky. She was at the bar with a girlfriend when said girlfriend spilt her drink – probably with a helpful nudge from him. Anyway, it gave him the chance to step in and buy a replacement. There's more to it, but that's the gist of what he told me. Love found a way.'

'A lot to digest in one evening.'

'Not one evening, no,' Peter said. 'I learned some things for the first time this afternoon. And then there were the occasions he and I bumped into each other after that first meeting, always in The Swan, of course. He'd be waiting for her and I'd have gone in for an early drink. I'm giving you a brief report stitched together from several meetings we had that winter and spring, all of them casual. He'd be keen to buy me a drink, and though I usually managed to turn him down I didn't want to hurt his feelings, especially when it became clear that Paddy really did love him. The way they looked at each other, touched, laughed ... it was love, right enough. Though there was no further mention of marriage. Loving in the present. Leaving the rest until she'd got her degree.'

Peter stopped his narrative, wriggled his shoulders, yawned. 'Anyway, by and large I took care to keep well clear of them. A nod, a wave, and that was that. Should I have worried that he was keeping her from her books? No, because he wasn't, at least I couldn't see any evidence to that effect. As I've said, her essays were always first class, her contributions in tutorials were as good as ever – if anything, better. She was, as the phrase goes, a high flyer and she stayed aloft. To be honest, I think their relationship was good for both of them. Love was not a hindrance.'

Coming round to Peter's side of the table, Susan stood behind her husband, folded her arms round his neck and nuzzled his ear as she said, 'But what did she see in *him*?' And, answering her own question, 'It *must* have been love. The weird emotion that led me to you, when I could have had my pick of – of traffic policemen, ice-cream sellers ... '

'Night soil men?' Peter suggested, turning in his chair to look up at her.

'I'm not sure I know what a night soil man is,' Susan said ruminatively, 'but it sounds not quite nice or proper. Not the kind of thing a well brought up young lady should know about. Like a professor. Ugh.'

And as they made their way upstairs they tried out other reprehensible titles. 'Politician, Praetorian, Pedant, Populator ... '

'That sounds good,' Susan said as she opened the bedroom door. 'Populator. I'll go for that.'

4

NEXT MORNING OVER BREAKFAST, SUSAN ASKED Peter more about DeVine's daughter. 'Did he tell you what she's studying?'

'Cultural Geography,' Peter said.

Susan paused in the act of reaching for the marmalade. 'Lordy,' she said, 'and here was I thinking that Geography was all about maps.'

Peter said, laughing, 'Geography's come a long way since you were nobbut a student, in those good old days, Gran, when History was chaps and Geography was, as you say, maps. Nowadays it spreads wide, hoovers up plenty of territory. Sociology, politics, earth sciences, anthropology, climatology, geology, and for all I know, night soil filtration.'

Nibbling at her toast, Susan said, 'So what is Cultural Geography?'

'I'll get her to tell me.'

Looking enquiringly at him, Susan said, 'You're planning to meet her then?'

'I'm in no hurry, but yes, I thought of sending a message to her via her department, explaining who I am and suggesting we might have coffee together some fine day.'

Then, seeing her doubtful expression, he asked, 'Why? What's the harm in that? She's free to say no, or simply ignore the suggestion.'

Susan emptied her coffee cup, re-filled from the cafetière, held it up enquiringly to him, and, as she poured for her husband, said, 'It's pretty weird, if you ask me. DeVine wants you to keep an eye on his daughter. What's he afraid of? That she might fall for some out-of-town rogue, for DeVine Mark 2. Like mother, like daughter? Is that it?' She leaned across the table, laid a finger on her husband's lips. 'Careful you don't get too involved.'

Peter laughed, took her hand and kissed it. 'I'm not an out-of-town rogue,' he said.

'And I'm an onlooker in this, I know, but DeVine's request – it, well, it strikes me as some way beyond the call of duty. I mean, you're not a friend of his, you don't owe him anything.'

And when he didn't answer, Susan said, her voice questioning, reasonable, 'Well, *do* you?'

Peter sat, face averted for some moments, then, turning to her, he said, 'Did I ever tell you about a boy I was at school with? Benjy Hall, he was called.'

Susan looked at him, puzzled. 'If you did I certainly don't remember. Should I?'

'No.' Peter was apologetic. 'No, I don't suppose I did mention him. In fact my own memories of him only re-surfaced last night.' He paused, emptied his cup, asked, 'Any more coffee?'

Susan looked, shook her head. 'I can make some more.'

'No, don't bother. I drink too much of the stuff, anyway.' He got up, walked across to the kitchen sink, poured himself a glass of water, and, as Susan stood to clear the breakfast things, Peter, leaning against the sink, said, 'I'll do those. You're due at school, aren't you?'

'On a Saturday?'

'Oh, lordy, I'm losing my marbles. Saturday, of course. Sorry, the events of the last twenty-four hours have been a bit discombobulating.'

'As they say down at the old Bull and Bush.'

Watching Peter's rueful smile, Susan, going up to him, pinched his cheek, kissed him lightly on the lips, and said, 'So you see, you have plenty of time to tell me about this Benjy Hull.'

'Hall. Benjy Hall.' He thought for a moment, said, 'It won't take long. There isn't much to tell.'

'So tell me. And while you're talking I'll brew some more coffee.'

'Good idea,' Peter said, and told her.

When he had finished and they were both once again sitting at the kitchen table, each with a fresh cup of coffee, Susan asked him, 'And you've never seen him since?'

'Since he left at the end of fifth form? No.'

'Poor lad,' Susan said. 'I wonder what happened to him.'

'I should have wondered at the time,' Peter said, staring into his cup. 'But I was going into the sixth form, new lands to conquer, and I suppose he went off to do his National Service. Some boys came back to see teachers they'd liked, who'd been helpful to them, but I can't imagine he'd have done anything of that sort.'

'And he had no friends?'

'Not at school, not so far as I recall. I don't think he knew anyone much to talk to, let alone befriend or be befriended by. He'd sometimes sit with a group of us at breaktime, though never at dinner. For that, he went back home – I mean to where he lived. And during break he'd look on at the rest of us while we talked and larked about. It was as though he was trying to understand us, as though we came from a foreign country, one whose ways were beyond him. I remember that on one occasion someone had got hold of an old, punctured football, and we sat in a ring, chucking it from one to another, trying to catch out anyone who wasn't expecting the ball to come to him. Plenty of laughs and jeers, of course, but Benjy took it all seriously. Whenever the ball came his way he'd be waiting for it and, when we cheered, he'd flush with pleasure. But he didn't join in the laughter. It was as if he was waiting to be invited to be part of a ritual he didn't understand. In wet weather he never came onto the grass. I guess he felt he mustn't get his clothes muddy. And at the end of the school day he'd go to the cloakroom, collect his raincoat, and walk out of school on his own, always on his own, back to the Barnardo's building at the far end of town. We found out that that was where he lived, so of course we never asked him about family, parents or brothers and sisters.'

They sat in silence for some minutes, and then Peter said, 'You'd have thought that one of us at least would have wanted to be his friend. He wasn't a freak of nature, not a helpless dumbo, in fact I remember he always did pretty well in end of term exams. But I don't think anyone got close to him. He never came to parties. It was as if the mark of Cain was on him.'

'And you're wondering whether this Benjy Hall is at all like DeVine – or vice versa.'

Peter nodded but did not speak.

'Why? Because both were – are – orphans?'

Again, Peter nodded.

'It's dreadful, isn't it,' Susan said. 'The war must have made orphans of so many kids.'

'Yes, of course,' Peter said. 'But these are two I know about, though in Benjy Hall's case I know precious little.'

He looked up, met his wife's gaze. 'What I *do* know, beyond doubt, is that both of them had to manage without love in their early lives. And that must have marked them – no, more than marked them, become part of them, of how they coped with being alive.'

'Which is why you're prepared to give DeVine the time of

day, do his bidding over this student, though in her case you seem to be wanting to spare her from repeating her mother's mistake. "Whatever you do, I beg you not to fall for the charms of a salesman, my dear young lady." How's that for irony.'

Peter got to his feet. 'Put that way it sounds ridiculous,' he said. 'But of course it isn't like that, as I now realise.'

He carried the used crockery over to the sink. Testing the water until it ran hot, he piled cups and saucers into the washing-up bowl while he said, 'This is how I see the matter. Anxious father wants to make amends, as he thinks, for being absent from his daughter's early years, and hopes to show his love for her, if in no other way than by trying to guard her from errors into which she might possibly fall.'

He stirred up the water into a soapy froth, began to wash the plates, devoting himself to careful inspection of the work in progress.

But Susan, coming up behind her husband, said, 'I could offer you a very different explanation for Mr DeVine's chivalrous intent.'

After a moment, during which Peter concentrated on what was in front of him, she said, 'Call me a cynic, but I'd say he's more likely to be after her money.'

And as Peter, shaking his head in vehement protest at her words, turned to her, she took a step backward and said, 'It's a reasonable hypothesis, admit. After all, this Patricia Connor must be something of an heiress, mustn't she, due to come into a fair sum of money when her grandparents pop their clogs – or espadrillos? Anyway, that's DeVine's assumption, so I'd guess. Keep her in your sights and hope that in the end she'll put some money in your pocket.'

'That's horrible,' Peter said.

'But conceivable.'

After a pause she added, 'Women learn to be suspicious of men's honourable intentions.'

'Balls,' Peter said. 'It isn't like that, not at all.' Calming down, he said, 'DeVine's doing pretty well for himself. He isn't a salesman, not any longer. My guess is that as a tax adviser he's beginning to make good money, and judging from his car and the way he dresses, there's now plenty in the bank. And quite apart from that, he'd never want to play foul by Paddy. He'd never do anything to hurt or offend *her* memory. The memory of the woman he loved.'

'She's dead,' Susan said.

Peter shook his head. 'Not to him, she isn't,' he told her.

5

'HE'S AFTER HER MONEY.'

At stray, unpredictable moments throughout the following week, Susan's words came unbidden into Peter's head. *Could* that be the explanation for DeVine's anxious plea for Peter to 'keep an eye' on Patricia? But no. DeVine would know that the girl's grandparents were far too shrewd to leave her money without written conditions, chief of which would certainly be that in no circumstances was her father to be allowed near any part of her inheritance. Anyway, he was becoming increasingly certain that DeVine's concern for his daughter was one of disinterest. He wasn't cynically playing the part of anxious parent, he *was* that parent.

But then at some point another obvious question thrust itself into his mind. Pat who? DeVine had never given him the young woman's surname. Her mother and DeVine weren't married after all, nor had her father played more than a bit part in the girl's upbringing. It was, he realised, far more likely she'd been given her mother's name, which was after all her grandparents' name, too. And what was that? For a panicky moment his mind was blank. Then it came to him. Connor. Of course. He would have to contact the Geography Department and ask if among their first-year students they had a Patricia Connor on their books. He assumed she was in her first year. If DeVine was so anxious to keep tabs on her he'd hardly have left contacting Peter for a whole year before he chose to get in touch.

Or would he? Suppose something had happened to make the man suddenly anxious about his daughter and her presumed fortune? Suppose, for instance, she'd met someone – a fellow student – with whom she'd fallen in love and who might himself be planning to get his hands on her money? But how would said student know that Patricia Connor was an heiress, or anyway had money in the bank, oodles of it? Because she'd told him? Oh, and when, where, why? Easy. They'd met at a student party, one at which Pat had got drunk and, in an effort to keep the attention of a youth to whom she was impulsively attracted, had revealed all.

Peter was in his university study when this fantasy of an imbroglio came to him. It had all the makings of a Jacobethan tragedy, he thought wryly. Young love destroyed by the evil wiles of an older relative, one who wants to get his hands on the fortune that belongs to his innocent niece, or in this case, daughter. A dagger, a poison phial. Death and Damnation. The DeVine Comi-Tragedy. Ho-ho. But no, put such thoughts behind thee. He ought to phone the Geography Department, find out whether they had a student who answered to the name of Patricia Connor.

He reached for his phone. Fortunately, he and Jim Hobbs – Professor Hobbs, known to all as Jack – were good friends, brought together by, among other interests, a passion for cricket. No, Jim had admitted, he was not a descendant of the great man, but he *had* been born in Surrey and from boyhood was a regular attender at the Oval. 'You may call me Hobbes,' Jim had said from the early days of their friendship. 'With an e.'

'And you're at liberty to call me Randall,' Peter replied, naming his favourite among contemporary batsmen. And so they did.

Now, as he lifted the earpiece, Peter almost without thought, identified himself as Randall to Jim's secretary. 'Good morning, Professor Randall,' the secretary who was in on the joke replied, adding that Professor Hobbs was away from the university until the following week, though if she could be of help she would be delighted to assist Professor Randall in any enquiries he might wish to pursue.

Professor Randall explained that he wished to ascertain whether a young lady called Patricia Connor was registered as a student with the Geography Department.

The secretary would consult the relevant lists in an attempt to answer Professor Randall's enquiry, though before she did so felt bound to enquire whether he wished to bowl the maiden over. Professor Randall laughed dutifully and went on to explain the reason for his enquiry.

'Her mother was a student in the English Department some twenty years ago,' Peter said. He hoped this would be sufficient explanation for his enquiry, and Professor Hobbs' secretary, who was most helpful, would now endeavour to answer Professor Randall's query. Should she phone him back or would he prefer to wait.

'I'll wait,' Peter said, and a few minutes later he learnt that Patricia Connor was indeed registered in the department as a student, one who had opted to study Cultural Geography, although in her first term she would, in common with all the other newcomers, be required to attend tutorials on the subject of geography as an academic discipline, and would be under the tutelage of Professor Hobbs himself.

Professor Randall thanked the secretary for her kindness and rang off.

But what, Peter wondered as he set the receiver back in its cradle, had his call achieved. Not much. He now knew that Pat Connor was here, at the University, and that she was indeed registered as a student in the Department of Geography. But that was the sum of his knowledge. He didn't know what she looked like, had no idea whether she lived in hall or digs, nor could he be at all certain of the best way to get in touch with her, or, supposing she agreed to see him, what on earth he could say to her. How was he to explain why he wanted to talk to her? 'Hullo, I used to teach your mother.' Hardly enough to guarantee the propriety of their meeting. Professor invites a first-year student to join him for a coffee in one of the campus bars on the pretext that some twenty years previously he had tutored her mother. Not good. And of course he couldn't mention the true reason for his wanting to make contact. That DeVine had asked him to do so. He surely couldn't mention her father, because that would entail explaining how he came to know him, which would in all probability lead at last to discussion of her mother's death. Supposing she asked him what he knew about the circumstances surrounding it, how much could he afford to say? He could, of course, tell her that he knew about that death and was extremely sorry for the unlooked-for demise of so gifted a student. He might even risk telling her something of the contents of her grandfather's letter accusing the University of dereliction of its duty, but that was all small beer and scarcely justified his proposing to meet Paddy Connor's daughter. Come to think of it, he didn't even know whether the young woman was aware of her mother's nickname, Paddy, the name by which her lover knew her. The young Patricia Connor had never *known* her mother, seen her, been nursed by her, been able to hear her voice. How terrible, Peter thought. To some degree, at least, she was, like her father, an orphan, though unlike him she had grandparents to care for her. Peter hoped they showed her some love, which, until Paddy Connor appeared as a bright star in his firmament, was more than DeVine had ever experienced, or, of course, Benjy Hall.

At home that evening, Peter made haste to tell Susan that he now knew for sure that Patricia Connor was a student in the University's Geography Department, and to his relief Susan nodded but didn't enquire any further. She was fully engaged in last-minute preparations concerning the school concert, which he'd naturally committed himself to attend. 'And Sally has said she'll be coming, too,' Susan told him. 'Not Paul, though. He and Gordon have a prior engagement.'

'But he's known for months about the concert.'

Susan eyed him, resignedly. 'I think their relationship may be at some sort of crisis point,' she said. 'They're trying to work it out, or work through it, as the marriage counsellors say.'

'It's not as if they're married.'

'True. And let's hope that makes separation easier.'

He risked saying, 'Let's also hope that it's an amicable parting of the ways. No worse cause.'

'I'm sure they take good care of themselves.' She hesitated. 'And each other.'

Her smile flickered then sprang to life. 'But Sally will be bringing someone she calls a "fella" with her. She sounded very pleased with herself. Fingers crossed this one will last.'

'Assuming he's not after her fortune.'

'The Simpson millions,' Susan said, 'prey to many a fortune-hunter,' and she laughed. But the laughter stopped short, and from her sudden look of guilty contrition, he knew that it wasn't her own daughter she was thinking of.

'I'll have to set up a meeting with Patricia Connor soon,' Peter said, 'I don't want DeVine breathing down my neck.'

'Wear a tight-fitting polo-neck,' Susan advised. 'That way you won't feel a thing.'

6

THE CONCERT WAS OVER AND PERFORMERS and invited guests crowded into the school staff room for coffee and sandwiches. In one corner a few bottles of wine stood on a small table spread with a stiff white cloth, and round it school governors and some city notables in chains of office made awkward conversation while they watched one of the more junior teachers haul at a corkscrew in an attempt to open bottles. The Head Teacher, in academic gown and hood, was, Peter noticed, introducing Susan to the city's Mayor, who stood ramrod straight as he offered her his congratulations. 'Splendid show,' he said, 'splendid show.' Then, as though fearing his words had been somehow inappropriate or insufficient, he added, 'Frightfully good.'

'We're all very pleased to have Susan with us,' the Head told him. 'Samples of her work have received public performance.' And she nodded gravely to indicate the significance of having a music teacher of such stature on her staff.

The Mayor gravely nodded back. 'Splendid show,' he said to Susan. 'Frightfully good.'

Who writes his script, Peter wondered.

He raised a sympathetic eyebrow to Susan but she was now being addressed by a grey-haired, portly Suit, so he turned away in the hope of locating someone he could talk to, and as he did so Simon Tims came limping toward him.

'Thank god for a friendly face,' Tims said *sotto voce* as he manoeuvred himself into position to stand toe to toe with Peter. Leaning close, he added, 'I'm only here because the wife couldn't come. I left her in bed with a filthy cold. So here I am. Behold the Man. Someone had to be in the audience to cheer on our two.'

'Our two' were twin sisters, who'd arrived at the school as Peter's own daughter, having completed her seven years there, was about to begin an undergraduate course in Librarianship at a Northern university. Tims now asked about Sally. 'She did well, didn't she? Got a good degree. I always think of women librarians as clad in cardies and sporting a lorgnette, but I don't see Sally as anything like that.'

'She's in post at one of the London colleges,' Peter told him, 'and enjoying life.' Standing on tiptoe he made a further attempt to look round the crowded room. 'She's somewhere in the crowd,' he explained, 'unless she and her partner have slipped out.'

'Can't say I'd blame them,' Tims said. 'No offence, but I'd rather be downing a pint in The Swan than standing here. However, I'm honour bound to see our two safely home. Bodyguard appointed to keep them protected from the lecherous young swarming through the Saturday night streets.'

Peter looked down at Tims' leg. 'You look as though you need a bodyguard yourself,' he said. 'What happened?'

'Did it in training,' Tims said. 'Turned the ankle over and it hurts like buggery. Even more of a pain than having to listen to that rock group, The Blowbacks, or whatever they call themselves.'

'Blowhards,' Peter corrected him. 'They weren't too bad, I thought. Showed clear evidence of knowing more than one key and three chords, unlike the skiffle groups of our own misspent youth.'

'Speak for yourself,' Tims said. 'Cliff was my hero. Britain's answer to Elvis.'

They laughed together before Tims, wincing as he began to shuffle away, said, 'This bloody ankle. I've had to pull out of the next couple of games. I guess there's nothing for it but to limp along to the staff meeting and offer Hetherington my considered views on our beloved department.'

'It's been cancelled. Didn't you know? I thought we'd all had the message. You should look more often in your in-tray.'

Tims ignored the suggestion. '*Cancelled?* I make myself available by going under the heels of some hairy son of the soil, and then Buggerlugs goes and cancels. Why, may I ask? To spite me? '

'According to his secretary he has to be away for the day. An urgent meeting in London. Sorry to spoil your pleasure. Still, it'll give you more time to get fit for your next sporting appearance.'

Peter shook his head, tut-tutted. 'Perhaps it was a warning. Ancient limbs. Have you thought it might be time to hang up your boots? I mean a man of your age ... '

'Forty-five,' Tims said, 'and I'll have you know that Stanley Matthews was still playing professional football at the age of fifty.'

'And apparently everyone had been warned against tackling him. He might have fallen to pieces.'

'You wouldn't get that consideration from the Ilkeston lot. Murderous buggers, the lot of them. Learnt their football from men like Chopper Harris.'

And again they laughed.

Later in the evening, as Peter and Susan linked arms and strolled home through a mild autumn evening, he asked her how she thought the concert had gone.

'How did *you* think it went? After all, you were audience.'

'Pretty good, wasn't it? That piece you wrote for the choir was excellent, everybody enjoyed that, you could tell by the warmth of the applause. Even the Mayor managed to stay awake up. The soloists were right up to the mark, and the chorus was spot on. No raggedy moments, none that I could detect, anyway.'

'No, they were good,' Susan agreed, 'I was proud of them all.'

The choir had sung her setting of a love song of John Clare's, and as she and her husband turned into the avenue that would bring them to their own house, Susan, her voice that deep contralto Peter so loved, sang some of the ballad's words.

'I would steal a kiss but I dare not presume,
Wert thou but a rose in thy garden sweet fairy,
And I a bold bee for to rifle its bloom,
A whole Summer's day would I kiss thee, my Mary!'

Peter opened the gate then spun round and put his arms round his wife. 'May I presume to steal a kiss,' he said.

'You may, kind sir,' Susan said, 'though a whole summer's day of them may not be possible.'

'Why no, 'tis autumn.'

'And I need a pee.'

As they broke apart, Peter, lifting his head to face the house, said 'Sally and Mark must be back. I turned the lights off before we left.'

A moment later he was opening the front door and as the two of them stepped inside they heard the sound of music coming from the rear of the house.

'It is your music, lady of the house,' Peter said, though before he had finished speaking Susan was running upstairs and a young dark-haired woman now stood in the hall, looking in some surprise and concern at her disappearing mother and then her father.

'Have you two had a row?' she asked him.

Peter's laugh was almost a shout. When he could control himself, he said to his daughter, 'No, dear Sally, quite the opposite. Hark.'

From above them came the sound of the lavatory flush. 'Your mother was taken short, which was why she was galloping upstairs as you came on the scene and this she will now avouch.'

He moved to the foot of the stairs and bowed low as Susan, descending, placed a hand on his head and said, 'My faithful servant.'

'At your service,' Peter said. He took his wife's hand and kissed it. 'Yum, yum,' he said.

'Well, if you haven't had a row you must have been drinking,' Sally said, laughing. 'Mark,' she called out, 'come and see this.'

The young man who came to join them, in jacket, jeans, and roll-neck navy-blue sweater, was smiling, hesitant but in no sense shy.

Sally put an arm round his waist as she introduced him to her parents.

Handshakes having been exchanged, 'Let's go into the front room,' Peter suggested, 'sit and relax.'

'You three do that,' Sally said, 'get to know each other while I make coffee for us all.'

So they did.

7

THE FOUR OF THEM WERE AT breakfast the following morning – 'blithely breakfasting all' as Peter put it – when the phone rang.

'On a Sunday morning,' Susan said, 'who on earth can *that* be?'

Sally pushed back her chair and stood. 'I'll go,' she said. 'I'll take it in your study, Dad, though it's probably someone wanting to congratulate Mum on last night's concert. Shall I put them onto you or are you not in this morning?'

She was back almost immediately. 'Dad, it's for you. Someone called DeVine, Terry DeVine. I told him I wasn't sure where you were but I'd try to find you. Are you in or out?'

'Tell the man your father's nowhere to be found.'

'No point,' Peter said, getting to his feet. 'Do that and he'll go on phoning until he's finally got me. I'd rather get it over and done with.'

As the others went on with their breakfasts and Susan poured more coffee for the three of them, she provided her daughter with a cursory explanation for DeVine's connection to her father.

It wasn't much and Sally looked suitably mystified but said nothing while Mark went on slowly crunching his way through a piece of toast.

'Well?' Susan asked when Peter re-appeared.

Meeting the challenge of her gaze, he said, 'He'll be passing through on Friday and wants to know whether we can meet for lunch.'

'And of course you said no.'

Resuming his seat as he reached for his cup, he said, 'And of course I said yes.'

'But why? Why not tell him you're busy, that you'll be in Timbuctoo, that you expect to fall under a bus ... ' Susan's words were accompanied with an exasperated shake of the head.

'Please, Miss, can we be told what this is all about,' Sally asked, and Susan, looking directly at Peter, said, '*You* tell them. Perhaps either Mark or Sally can help.'

So Peter told them.

When he had done, Sally said, 'Wow, it's a bit difficult to take in first time around.' She put a hand on Mark's shoulder. 'Did you follow all Dad's story?'

'I got the gist of it,' Mark said.

'And?'

Mark looked across the table at Peter, then, to Susan, he said, 'You're worried this Mr DeVine may be something of a fortune hunter – after his daughter's money?'

'He's not, I'd swear to it,' Peter said.

'He just wants someone to lurv.'

Peter shook his head and his pursed lips indicated an implicit rebuke of Sally's flippant remark.

'He's pushy, he doesn't have much by way of social grace –'

'But,' Susan said, cutting off Peter's words, 'your dad puts his faults down to the fact that he was born an orphan. A foundling,' she added.

'Having to fight for his place in the sun,' Mark said, looking round the table. 'I can understand that.'

As though detecting from the wry tone of his words an emphasis hidden from her parents, Sally turned to look concernedly at her lover. 'You were an only child,' she said, 'weren't you? Your parents doted on you.' She leant her head on his shoulder. 'Can I tell Mum and Dad about it?'

'As you wish,' Mark said. He sat back in his chair, put his hands flat on the table either side of his plate, and Susan thought he wasn't keen that Sally should do so. As though recognising the same thing, but plainly wanting a justification for what she was about to reveal, Sally said, partly to him and also to her parents, 'It was a long time ago.' But, as though uncertain whether to continue, she stopped there. Squeezing his hand, 'You ought to tell them,' she said, 'it's your story.'

'My parents were killed in a plane crash. That's it. End of story.'

Mark picked up his knife, stared at its blade for some moments then said, without looking at any of his listeners, his voice now oddly formal, as though he was making a statement, 'My father had to go to Corsica on business and he took my mother with him. Monday to Friday, that was the arrangement. And while they were gone I went to stay with a family nearby. I was friends with the two boys, we all went to the same school, and their parents were friendly with mine.'

He lifted his head. 'All good friends and jolly good company. Ha, ha.'

Into the silence that followed, he spoke again. 'I was ten at the time,' he said, as though completing his statement. 'There, now I've told you all you need to know.'

A further silence. 'I'm so sorry,' Susan finally said. She raised her eyes, wanting to meet Mark's, but he was still studying his knife. He nodded in acceptance of her words, shrugged.

'Ah well, as Sally says, it was a long time ago. Getting on for twenty years.'

Peter said, 'About the same time as Paddy Connor's death.'

To her parents, Sally said, perhaps wanting to change the subject, 'I thought I'd take our guest up to the woods at Slaney.' She shook her head in mock disbelief. 'Can you imagine? Three years a student and I doubt he knows what trees look like. As far as I can discover this young man hardly ever strayed off campus. Did you?' she asked, turning to speak exclusively to him.

He held up his hands in a gesture of confession. 'Guilty as charged,' he said.

'And do you have anything to say in your own defence?' Peter asked, smiling.

'Couldn't be separated from my books,' Mark said.

'Rubbish.' Sally flapped a hand in dismissal. 'On the sports field all day and in the bar all night.'

'Chance would be a fine thing,' Mark said, stroking her hair. Levering himself up from the table, he said to his hosts, 'Leave us to clear away the breakfast things, please.'

But Peter was emphatic. 'Certainly not. Out into the sun, both of you. And don't return until dinner is on the table, one-thirty. That will leave plenty of time to put you on a late afternoon train. You'll be back in the Wen by seven o'clock.'

'The Wen,' Sally said, herself now standing, and laughing at her lover's puzzled expression. 'London. So called, apparently, by Cobbett.' And before Mark could ask her how she came by that piece of information, she said, 'Dad told us that when we were little. As a way of warning us off imagining that London's streets were paved with gold. Didn't do any good, though, did it. Paul and I are both there.'

'And me,' Mark said.

'And you,' Sally said, 'thank goodness.' And hooking an arm round his neck, she kissed him full on the lips.

***

'They seem happy enough,' Peter said as he and Susan cleared the table. 'Do we hope it lasts?'

'We do,' Susan said. 'He's certainly an improvement on her previous lovers. And for a research chemist he's surprisingly presentable.'

'What were you expecting? Someone in a torn lab coat smelling of formaldehyde?'

'Anything rather than the last one. Leathers and a bike and beyond talk of ton-ups he didn't seem interested in *anything.*'

'He wasn't that bad,' Peter said, laughing. 'But our Sally does rather pick 'em.'

As he began to stack the breakfast plates, Susan said, 'Anyway, research chemists don't smell of formaldehyde.'

'They don't?'

'No,' Susan said. 'I once had to be near to Thatcher when she came to school to tell us all about her achievements at university and as Minister of Education. She studied chemistry, you know.'

'I do know,' Peter said. 'And what did she smell of?'

'Sulphur,' Susan said. 'Definitely.'

***

Over the following days, they found themselves on several occasions discussing their daughter and her relationships. None had proved at all long lasting, until, that is, Mark came into her life.

One evening, as they stood in the kitchen, their meal at an end, Peter asked Susan whether Sally had told her mother anything about how she and Mark met.

'It was a re-meeting,' Susan told him. 'Apparently they knew each other from university days. One of those casual acquaintances that happen to all students. Too casual to be kept up once you've gone your different ways.'

'I never heard her mention his name when she was in Manchester,' Peter said, before acknowledging to himself that Sally wasn't the kind of daughter who would be likely to keep her parents closely informed about her undergraduate life. 'Did she mention him to you?'

'I think so,' Susan said, 'but I can't really remember. She was friendly with a wide number of male students, though she always stressed to me that they were more by way of passing acquaintances. From what she said I imagine that she and Mark bumped into each other at parties but no more than that. "Hello, how are you?", "Nice weather for the time of year", that kind of meaningless chat. It was London that brought them together, and that was by pure chance. Sally told me that he came into her library one day when she was on the front desk. He was in search of a book, they recognised each other, got talking – "Well, well, fancy seeing you here" – and I don't know much more than that, you'll have to imagine it for yourself.'

'He asked her out for a coffee,' Peter said, picking up his cue, 'their hands touched as they reached for the sugar, a spark flew between them ... '

'You should have been a novelist,' Susan said, holding out a teacloth, 'now, do your duty, husband, dear.'

'Or perhaps it was a cocktail bar,' Peter said, as he began to dry plates. Seeing Mark and Sally together had given him a sudden jolt of happiness. 'The kind of bar,' he went on, 'where the lights are low, a piano tinkles in a corner, and a swarthy barman mixes gin and beer ... '

'Gin and beer !'

'They were fresh out of rum,' Peter said. 'And anyway there was no ice that evening. Gin and beer was all that was available.'

'But little they recked, having eyes for themselves alone.'

'Eyes for each other, surely.'

'Pedant,' Susan said. And as they heard the phone ring, she ordered, 'If that's DeVine tell him, please, to get lost.'

But it wasn't DeVine. 'Hi,' Paul's voice said, when Peter picked up the receiver. 'Dad? Is Mum there?'

Some twenty minutes later, when Susan came back into the kitchen where Peter sat, at his elbow a fresh-brewed pot of coffee, she dropped into her chair, and as he looked enquiringly at her, 'It seems that once again Paul's on his own,' she said. 'His chief reason for phoning was to apologise to me for not being at the concert – he says he's sent a letter though it won't have arrived yet. But he also wanted to tell me that he'd like to come up sometime soon, for a weekend. 'On my own,' he said, 'by choice.''

'Good,' Peter said. 'In fact, very good.'

But Susan, as she sipped her coffee, said, 'He sounded not at all happy. Didn't you think so?'

'We only exchanged a word or two,' Peter said. 'Not enough to tell.'

'Umm.' Susan drained her cup, reached for the coffee pot, and then returned it to the table without re-filling either of their cups. 'I hope he's alright,' she said. Then, speaking with determined brightness, 'Anyway, it will be good to see him.' And Peter, studying her half-closed eyes, the lower lashes on which tears trembled, realised yet again how dearly she loved their selfish, self-centred son, the son he, too, loved. And perhaps, after all, Paul wasn't so much self-centred as understandably self-protective. It might sound the same thing, but it wasn't, not at all. He wished he could say this to Paul himself. Perhaps when his son – *their* son – was with them they could find a way to discuss the matter.

8

THURSDAY EVENING. PETER WAS ALONE. HE and Susan had eaten early so that, having grabbed her cello from the hall, she could rush out to rehearse with The Clifton String Quintet, and having cleared away the dinner things, he was planning to spend the evening with a new study of late nineteenth century literature. It was billed as a post-structuralist 'intervention' and after ten minutes reading he was about to give up when the phone rang.

'Is that Professor Randall's habitation?'

'Am I speaking to Professor Hobbs?' Peter said, laughing. At least it wasn't DeVine.

'Right first time. I hear you've been enquiring after one of our first-year students. I take it that your intentions are honourable?'

'They most certainly are,' Peter said. 'Have you got a moment while I explain?'

'Feel free,' Jim Hobbs said. 'Though before you do so I'd better tell you that Ms Connor is away for a few days. A beginner's study tour of regional galleries, organised by Jill Dawson, lecturer in charge, Dr Dawson to you. Don't ask me the details of the itinerary, because I haven't a clue. And that said, you may now continue.'

Reaching for his half-empty wine glass, Peter gave his friend a bare-bones account of the brilliant Paddy Connor, her unexpected pregnancy, her trip to Hamburg with the father-to-be in order to meet – confront – her parents, her unlooked-for, tragic death, and her baby's survival.

'And the infant grew up to become the student now in my department,' Jim said. 'Am I right?'

'Got it in one,' Peter said, and told Jim as much as he knew about Patricia Connor's history, from her birth to her present circumstances.

'Sad story,' Hobbs said, when Peter had finished. 'I suppose we have to credit the grandparents for doing their best, according to their own lights at least; though scarpering off to Spain and leaving the girl to an aunt's tender mercies isn't my idea of parental responsibility.'

'A great-aunt in point of fact. Her grandmother's younger sister, though I expect she called her aunt. And of course they weren't her parents, though in her early years they acted as if they were.'

'Which is why they took care of her education, and from what you say it seems they were only too keen to keep her from her father's clutches.'

Peter set down his glass. 'I think – no, I'm sure – they saw him as a tin-pot rogue, a fly-by-night who got their daughter pregnant and couldn't be trusted to take care of her. They almost certainly blamed him for her death. Besides, he wasn't their "sort". I'm willing to bet they made enquiries and discovered he was a war orphan, a Foundling, himself a product of some fly-by-night shudder in the loins.'

'And now *her* daughter, this Patricia Connor, has become a student here.'

'It was apparently her own idea. She insisted on it, so I

gather. An act of remembrance, a way of honouring the memory of the mother she never knew.'

'Yes, I can understand that,' Jim said. 'But then why not become a student in your department?'

'Probably because she prefers Cultural Geography as an academic discipline. You ought to be proud, Professor Hobbs, rather than question her choice.'

Ignoring the tongue-in-cheek rebuke, Hobbs said, 'And you're alerting me to her presence, but why? So I can report back to you if I see her in the clutches of some undesirable male, yet a further fly-by-night?'

'I'm not begging any favours, Jim, promise. But I'd count it as an act of friendship if you'd let me know of any – anything about her behaviour that seems odd or ... ' Peter was unsure how to continue. 'The truth is,' he finally said, 'that her father wants to keep in touch with her. It's his way of forming some sort of bond, however slight, with his daughter. He's anxious, I suppose, to see that she comes to no harm.'

Again, he paused. 'Terry DeVine, he's called,' he added, feeling that this talk wasn't going as he'd hoped.

'It's a reasonable enough request,' Jim Hobbs said. 'In fact, I'd say it sounds entirely honourable. I can think of many men in his position who'd have taken to their heels. Happens all the time. And if they're nabbed by the law they pay some maintenance and count themselves lucky they don't have to marry the poor lass they got in the family way.'

'Put like that,' Peter said, 'I agree with you one hundred per cent.'

'But?'

'But she seems to have become something of an heiress. I don't know the ins and outs, not at all, though I *do* know that when her grandparents die – the ones who'd brought her back to England after her mother's death and are now sunning themselves in Spain – well, then, she's bound to come into a tidy sum of money. They've no one else to leave it to, so she stands to receive the lot. It's either that or a Dogs' home. I imagine the money is in a trust fund for her, and from what her father says he learnt from the great-aunt who's been looking after her in recent years that her grandparents are determined it doesn't go elsewhere, though I suppose auntie herself is in line for a penny or two if she survives. She's the grandmother's younger sister,' he added, 'I know that much and I also know that she loathes her brother-in-law. Got all that?'

'I think so,' Jim Hobbs said. 'And if I'm following you aright, you suspect that this Connor girl's father is somehow hoping to get his hands on her money.'

'*I* don't suspect that, but others do.' Peter chose not to mention Susan by name. 'DeVine has asked me to exercise some sort of watching brief over Patricia, which is why I'm mentioning all this to you now.'

'Blimey,' Jim said. 'A bit convoluted, if you don't mind my saying so. And what about the aunt, or great-aunt. Mightn't she want to be keeping a weather eye out for her charge?' He paused, then went on, 'That makes four by my count. Great aunt, DaVinci or whatever his name is, you, me. Four sets of beady eyes all fixed on the one young lady. Is anyone else in on the game?'

'I know, I know. What a rigmarole, as my old mum would have said.'

'Rigmarole is putting it mildly.'

'Well, no need to lose any sleep over all I've told you,' Peter said.

'I'll try not to,' Jim Hobbs said. 'How's Susan by the way. Keeping busy?'

'She's out at rehearsal with The Clifton String Quintet, preparing for their Christmas concert, and Sally was up at the weekend with her latest lover.' He decided not to mention Paul, and Hobbs didn't ask.

'You and Clarrie OK?' he asked.

'Fit as ever,' Jim Hobbs said, adding, 'It's high time we all met up for a meal.'

'It is and we must,' Peter said, and preparing to put down the phone, he said, 'Thanks, Jim, you've been a pal.'

But later, as he stood at the sink to wash out his glass, he wondered whether he'd done the right thing in telling his friend as much about DeVine as he'd felt obliged to do.

* * *

'Hi,' DeVine said, when, as agreed, they met at the saloon bar of The Swan the following lunchtime. 'By the way, I'm buying lunch, alright.'

He was wearing what looked to be a new, expensively tailored suit of dark grey wool with thin, faint blue stripes, and the button-down collar of his impeccably white shirt was set off by a slim maroon tie. The very image of a successful business man.

As they sat at the table DeVine had reserved for them, and after they'd ordered from the menu held out for their inspection by a waitress whom Peter guessed to be a moonlighting student, and each had asked for a pint of beer to go with their cod and chips, Peter asked what had brought DeVine up England on this occasion. DeVine told him that he'd been in Newcastle in his professional capacity and was now, after two days 'oop north' on his way back to London.

The beer arrived, they raised their glasses to each other, and Peter, having taken a first sip, asked DeVine, 'Before the conversation becomes general, as the saying goes, do you mind telling me what a tax adviser *is* exactly? I'm keen to learn. To be blunt, what do you do to make your money? I probably ought to know, but the truth is I haven't a clue. I assume you had to study tax matters somewhere?'

And when DeVine looked quizzically at him, he said in

self-defence, 'I'll be honest. I always thought you were a salesman, pure and simple.'

DeVine, leaning back in his chair, shook his head, his smile that of a man at his ease. 'Yup,' he said. 'That was me, alright, in previous years at least. On the road with my wares pure and simple as they come.'

But the smile went. Leaning forward, elbows on the table though not directing his gaze at Peter, he said, 'Truth is, after Paddy's death I couldn't get my head straight for a long, long time. I went on flogging goods for the same firm but business was dropping off. Many once-open doors were closing and there was nothing I could do about it. In the end the firm told me they'd have to let me go, and I can't say I blamed them. I was bloody useless. And of course, Paddy's death was always on my mind. The fact that I hadn't been with her at the end, hadn't seen my own – *our* own – child, hadn't been at the funeral, hadn't even been told when it was; *and* was being squeezed out by her bloody parents. It all got to me.'

He studied the place mat in front of him. 'It was a bad, bad time,' he said. 'No work, no incentive, too much drink.'

Then, 'Anyway, to cut to the chase, I pulled myself together, changed digs by way of making a new start, and decided to try for some other career. I'd a bit of money saved for when Paddy and me would be married and together, and a drinking pal asked why didn't I apply for accountancy work.' He looked at Peter. 'Good with figures, I was – am. I thought he must be joking, but he put me in touch with someone who was an accountant, I got taken on as a trainee in his company, passed some exams, and there, minus several chapters that would bore you to buggery, is the story of my life. Anyway, life as an accountant. A thrill a minute.'

'And a tax adviser?'

'That came out of accountancy work. I learnt the ropes and then decided to set up on my own. Believe it or not my previous occupation as traveller across all parts of England helped. Widely known as Trustworthy Terence. He will sort out your tax affairs. Leave it to him and you'll never again spend days worrying over demands for your hard-earned cash from the men in suits.'

'I never knew it could be so easy,' Peter said ironically, realising for the first time how far from easy the man sitting opposite him had found his life. A new respect for DeVine came to him, admiration, too. 'You've done well,' he said, and was at once ashamed of his words, their trivial import. Condescending bastard. 'Sorry,' he said.

Before DeVine could answer, plates of crinkly battered cod, chips and peas were placed in front of them.

'Mushy peas,' DeVine said, rubbing his hands as he did so. 'You can't get these in London, not like they do them up here. He examined the few that were impaled on his fork, before lifting them to his mouth. As he chewed he nodded contentedly. 'Smashing,' he said, using a word Peter would have least expected to hear from this smartly suited city gent sitting opposite.

'Yes,' he said, when he could again speak. 'A bit of bloody alright, I can tell you.' He grinned at Peter. 'See what being a tax adviser can get for you. Lunch at a leading hostelry in the company of a leading academic at a leading university.'

Peter played along. 'And the academic only too happy to be in the presence of a leading man in financial ... er, matters.'

They bent to their food.

But a few moments later, Peter having more or less cleared his plate while DeVine pushed his half-finished lunch to one side, he asked, 'Do you mind if we talk a bit about your daughter, Patricia? Patricia Connor, that is. I know she's kept her mother's name.'

'Connor was her grandfather's name, of course,' DeVine said. 'And Patricia was what they both decided on. If at first you don't succeed ... ' His mouth twisted in a thin smile.

'Naturally I was not consulted.' The smile vanished, as, with a flush of defiance, he said, 'But she's *my* daughter, for all they must wish she wasn't.'

He was silent for a moment, looking at his plate. Then raising his head, he said, 'My only child. I never got married, not after Paddy. No chance. I don't have any other kiddies. I'm on my ownio.'

He drank a good half of his pint, before, meeting Peter's gaze, he repeated, 'after Paddy ... ' He shook his head. 'There have been a few one-nighters, I'll admit, but nothing serious. Not after Paddy. Nothing.'

He reached for a chip which he chewed slowly, then, 'Truth is, I couldn't bear to think of anyone else as – well, as a lover, a wife.'

And Peter, noting the man's averted gaze, the awkward mix of comic bravado and hesitant candour, thought, he's telling the truth. All those years without her and she's still his only love.

He said, holding up his hand, awkward himself now, 'Confession time. I'm afraid I've still not found an occasion to meet your daughter, your Patricia.'

DeVine shrugged, but Peter could sense his disappointment. 'Ah, well, give it time,' was all DeVine found to say.

'I've talked to her head of department, though. A good friend, Jim Hobbs. He tells me that she's away from the University for a few days.'

DeVine looked at him enquiringly, puzzled, more likely sceptical, and Peter thought, perhaps he doesn't trust me. He thinks I'm not going to help him.

Anxious now to reassure the man sitting opposite, he said, 'Jim explained that Patricia's on a kind of introductory course – visits to museums, art galleries ... '

'But she's doing a Geography degree? What's that got to do with swanning off to galleries?'

As their plates were taken away, Peter, wanting to ease the sudden switch of mood said, 'It seems that Cultural Geography doesn't have much to do with maps or crops or – well, I guess that Geography has changed since our – since my – day. It's a cross between History and Art and Architecture. I'll be sure to ask your daughter when I can find an excuse to meet her. Promise.'

But DeVine wasn't mollified. 'Fancy anything else?' he asked brusquely, as the student waitress returned to stand by their table. 'Pudding, coffee?' The way he asked the question made plain that he still wasn't sure he could trust his guest. The brief accord between them had evaporated.

Peter shook his head. He drank the last of his beer, and, when he lowered his glass, watching as DeVine took the bill, reached for his wallet, put some notes into the waitress's tray, and waved away any suggestion of change, he said, 'Terry, it would help if you understood that I have to tread carefully as far as your daughter is concerned. Or rather, it would help if I knew how far you're prepared to let me know what kind of thing I can say to her. I can tell her that her mother was a student of mine, but so what? I mean, that's not much of a reason for suggesting we meet for – for a coffee, I suppose. Am I allowed to know the circumstances of her mother's death?'

'Why not,' DeVine said.

'You'd not mind?'

DeVine swilled round the remains of his beer glass, then swallowed the contents before saying, 'Anyway, she might not want to tell you.'

Briefly, he stared away before, looking back and almost, it felt, squaring up to Peter's gaze, he said, 'Truth is, I don't really know her. I've hardly ever been alone with her, she's more or less a stranger to me. Her damned grandparents did their best – worst – to make sure I saw as little of my daughter as they could. They were graciously prepared to permit me the occasional visit – *very* occasional – but I had to make the running, ask for an interview they weren't keen to encourage, I can tell you. A yob like me, who'd as good as killed their daughter, that was how I assumed they thought of me. So, short of making her a ward of court, once they were back in England they were stuck with me turning up on their doorstep – "by arrangement" – from time to time. I was never allowed inside, and no doubt the whole bloody place was fumigated as soon as I was off the premises. So we went for walks. She had some kind of nurse who came with us in her early years, then, when my little girl was older, a "companion" had to be in tow, to squash any plan I might have to abduct her. They even had a private detective hang around outside the gates of the posh school they sent her to, so I learned, in case I showed my unwashed face there. They could have saved their bloody money, of course. By then I was a working man, needing to earn my corn.'

'How do you know all that?' Peter asked him, following DeVine's actions as his host pushed back his chair and stood. 'I mean, if you *weren't* there, at the school gates, how could you know about the detective?'

DeVine laughed, a brief derisive sound. 'You're wondering how paranoid a man can get.'

His stare, one of near contempt, made clear the distance there now was between the two of them. 'Well, Professor Simpson, I have to tell you that I was the recipient of a letter in which they – *he* – gave me to understand that they would be taking steps to ensure Patricia Connor's continuing safety while she was receiving her education.'

And he turned to lead the way out of The Swan.

'They could have been bluffing.'

DeVine span round. 'The letter came from their Solicitor's office,' he said. 'On headed paper. Want to see it? Know for a fact I'm not inventing anything?'

And again he swung round, made for the pub's outer door.

As the two of them stood by DeVine's car in breezy autumnal sunlight, Peter said, 'Terry, I'm sorry about that. Truly sorry. I don't want my stupid remarks to have spoilt a lunch I very much enjoyed.'

He held out his hand, and, after DeVine had stared at it for a moment, he briefly shook it.

'Drive safely,' Peter said as the sleek car's door shut and DeVine made for the car park exit.

Peter waited and watched until the saloon disappeared, his hand raised in salutation.

To himself, he muttered, 'Idiot. *Idiot.* You nearly ruined that.'

* * *

He was still feeling an abashed guilt for his crass stupidity, when, some hours later, he sat opposite Susan, drinking tea and trying to explain all that had happened during his lunch with DeVine. He wanted to tell her he was pretty well certain that Patricia Connor's father had no plans for getting at her money, that DeVine was, in fact, an honourable man who wanted the best for his daughter, a daughter he loved for her mother's sake, the mother to whose dear memory he was honour-bound. But well before the end of what he'd been intending to tell his wife, he stopped. 'You're not listening,' he said.

'Sorry.' Her apologetic smile was perfunctory. 'I was thinking about Paul.'

'What about Paul?'

'I was thinking how dreadful it is being a parent, having to worry about not seeing your child. That man and his daughter ... '

'What's that got to do with Paul? Paul's our son and we love him and we're not kept from seeing him.'

'But I sometimes feel that I don't know anything about

him, about ... ' her voice trailed away, and he saw the tears in her eyes.

'His being homosexual – gay?' He reached across, took her hand which lay, unresisting, in his. 'He's been open about it for years now.'

'But this awful disease gay men are dying from. You *must* worry about that.'

'Of course I do. But Paul can take good care of himself.'

'You sound as though you think he's selfish.' And before Peter could reply she stood, as though determined to change the subject, and marched across to the kitchen counter.

'I'm going to make a sandwich for myself,' she said over her shoulder, 'before I go off to evening practice. Do you want me to make you one?'

The abruptness of her tone startled him. 'Not just now,' he said, 'I had a heavy lunch.'

'Please yourself,' she said.

It sounded, he thought, like an accusation.

9

'FAMILY VALUES,' PAUL SAID, 'LET'S NEVER forget family values.'

The three of them, Peter, Susan, and Paul himself, were sitting round the kitchen table drinking coffee that Peter had brewed in readiness for his son's arrival.

Susan, her eyes fixed on Paul's face, her smile widening, said, 'It's so lovely to see you look so ... '

'So normal?' he asked, laughing, 'So well? So average?' But there was no mockery in his voice.

Joining in his laughter, Susan said, 'So handsome.'

And in his jeans and black sweater, the longish, pale, clean-shaven face topped by a crop of near-black hair, Paul was, both his parents were happy to recognise, not merely good-looking, he exuded an air of relaxed confidence, of being at ease with himself and with them.

He had proposed they raise their cups in a tongue-in-cheek toast to 'Our beloved prime minister,' having on arrival picked up and read a leaflet which had earlier that morning been pushed through the letter-box. The leaflet, in blue lettering, proclaimed on behalf of the local Conservative Party, a forthcoming meeting at the Party Office where William Whitelaw, no less, would be speaking about 'Conservative Party Triumphs and Values', and rouse the faithful to vote in the forthcoming General Election.

'Has Kinnock a chance, do you reckon?' Susan now asked him.

Paul shrugged. 'I'm no expert in these matters. My landlady tells me, "They're All the Same, if you ask me. In it for Themselves." I wasn't asking her by the way. What do you think?'

Peter said, 'There are some positive signs. Simon Tims says he's going to stand as an independent "Bring Back the Birch" candidate. He says it will skim off half the local Tories, sneak Labour in by the back door – in our constituency, at least.'

'And who's Simon Tims when he's at home?' Paul asked, laughing.

'One of your father's colleagues,' Susan said. 'A specialist in early modern literature, isn't that right?' she asked Peter, who nodded. 'And an exponent of early modern football,' he added. 'Aka Batter and Clog. Known by his distinctive walk, a pronounced hobble.'

'In which case the Birchers will catch him and flog him to death.' Paul, pushing his chair back, stood, his slender frame suddenly imposing itself on his parents. 'Mind if I take myself upstairs for a wash and brush up? Three hours car travel on the Saturday motorway can leave a man feeling – well, battered and clogged.' And picking up his overnight bag he disappeared through the connecting door to the hall.

But his head immediately re-appeared. 'Same room?' he said.

Half turning toward him, Susan said, 'The same room as ever. *Your* room.'

She listened for her son's steps as they dwindled on the stairs, then, turning to Peter, she said, 'He's alright, isn't he?' And the choked relief in her voice squeezed his heart.

He nodded, not trusting himself to speak.

'I wonder why he made such a point of telling us he'd be on his own?' she said, as much to herself as to Peter.

'When was that?'

'Last time he phoned. To tell us he'd be coming this weekend.' She said, reprovingly, 'Your head's been so full of this DeVine business you haven't been able to spare a thought for your own son.'

'Not true.'

Pretending to consider her words, he said, 'At a guess, he didn't want to put us – you – to the chore of making up two beds.'

'More likely there's been a falling out with the one he'd been mentioning of late. Jimmie, wasn't it? Well, if you're single there's no rule that says you have to stay loyal to your love of the moment.'

'True, I suppose,' Peter said, thinking the words were an oddly cynical way of putting the matter. Or did Paul regularly up sticks and move on to pastures new? And as he thought that, so he thought of DeVine and of DeVine's strange – was it? – loyalty to the woman who had been dead for at least twenty years. Undying love? Or fixed obsession?

He took their cups over to the sink. He'd swill them out while Susan went upstairs to, in her own word, 'titivate' herself before the three of them went out to lunch at the nearby hotel where Peter had reserved a table.

His wife's suspicion as to DeVine's true motive for re-establishing contact troubled him more than he wanted to admit. That vow of undying love to Paddy Connor. Was DeVine trying to convince him, Peter, that he was the genuine, broken-hearted, once-in-a-lifetime lover? But why? Oh, so that Peter would, with luck, repeat his words to the daughter when she and Peter met. That would soften her up, so that her father, the man she scarcely knew, would become a man she could learn to trust. And from there proceed to the contents of her purse.

But no, he couldn't bring himself to believe that. It was downright ridiculous. Apart from anything else, DeVine didn't *need* money. He was now a successful man of business, he was doing OK. And his commitment to Paddy Connor's memory was, Peter had no doubt, while difficult to fathom, entirely genuine. As the cliché had it, his, DeVine's, was the love of a lifetime.

* * *

Nevertheless, Peter chose to discuss the matter with Paul and Susan over lunch. Paul, who knew nothing about his father's one-time student, would come to the story with an open mind. And it was to his son that Peter directed most of what he had to say. Over grilled dover sole, one of the restaurant's specialities and a favourite of Paul's, Peter told him about the twenty-year-old tragedy of Paddy Connor's death, making a good deal of DeVine's grief, his lasting determination to stay close to his daughter, despite her grandparents' best efforts to guard her against him, which involved the hire of a private detective to report on the girl's activities as she grew through her teenage years.

'But surely DeVine had some rights in the matter,' Paul protested. He slipped a morsel of fish into his mouth. 'Excellent, by the way. Feel free to pass my compliments to the chef.'

He laid down his fork in order to raise his glass of white wine. 'This Chablis is not to be sneered at, either, forsooth.'

Smiling at her son's evident pleasure in his meal, Susan asked, 'Don't they feed you in London, then?'

'I do most of my own cooking,' Paul said. 'Beans on toast with a dash of cinnamon a speciality, much commented on by friends and foes alike. The busy life of a social worker, you see. Not much time for slaving over a hot stove.'

Then, to his father, 'Sorry, Dad. You were saying ... '

'I was about to tell you that DeVine and Paddy's parents came to some sort of agreement about how often he'd be allowed to see her. They held all the cards. He was a near-penniless salesman, they were well-heeled, even wealthy.'

'So what happened? I'd like to hear.'

Ten minutes later, by which time Paul's plate was clean, Peter had told him of the Connors' return from Hamburg to their house in Highgate, of Patricia's being sent to the same schools her mother had attended, and then, when she was sixteen or so, of their swanning off to sunny Spain, leaving her to the care of her grandmother's sister ... though Patricia was, he thought, permitted an occasional visit to their hacienda, and from time to time one of them might take a plane to London.

Interrupting his father's narrative, Paul asked, 'And do they have any plans for their granddaughter's future?'

Peter shrugged. 'No idea,' he said. 'Perhaps their own daughter's fate – her death – has taught them some caution. Anyway, I can't imagine that DeVine will have heard anything. What I know is patched together from scraps he's produced, and most of that is, for all I know, surmise. My guess is that they've decided to leave her to take her chance. The sister will have kept them up to date with the girl's progress, and I imagine they think that they've done as much as can be expected of them to safeguard her future. They've had their fingers burnt once. Maybe they're content to be with the money and crooks downing sangria on an Iberian beach. Now, would you like any afters? Cheese? Pudding?'

'Eh?' Paul, who had been listening intently to his father's tale hadn't noticed the waitress who was standing silently beside him. Looking up at her, he said, 'Sorry, I didn't mean to be rude.' His quick, apologetic smile was as charming as it was sincere, Susan knew, knowing in the same instant how dearly she loved her son. Both she and Peter turned down the suggestion of more to eat, though she asked for coffee and Peter, plucking the bottle, now empty, from the ice bucket, wondered aloud whether anyone would like a brandy.

'Just coffee for me,' Paul said to the waitress, favouring her with another smile, and Peter, defeated, asked for three coffees. She blushed faintly as she turned away from Paul's smile, and Peter, noticing, exchanged glances with Susan.

'Anyway,' he said, picking up his story where it had been broken off, 'with the two grandparents now old, DeVine's daughter's as good as an heiress-in-waiting, or so I assume.'

'And you also assume that her father might want to get his hands on her fortune.'

'*I* don't. It's your mother who assumes that.'

Paul turned to her. 'Have you met him?' he asked her, then paused as their coffees arrived, together with a jug of cream. 'Sugar's on the table.' The waitress directed her words at Paul, who this time neither spoke nor smiled as he nodded his thanks.

'You've ruined her day,' Susan said, watching the young woman as she vanished through the kitchen's swing door.

Peter said quickly, 'Well, my son, what do you make of the story? And what would you advise me to do?'

After a moment or two, during which Paul, staring into his coffee cup, said nothing, he raised his head, met his father's questioning look, and said, 'I take it that all you've told me comes from what ... what Mr DeVine told *you*. Has he a first name, can I ask?'

'Terry,' Peter said, 'Terry DeVine. He's a man with what I think I can safely call a good career, a tax adviser. And yes, all I know comes from him, apart from the fact of his – of Paddy Connor's brilliance as a student. That, I know for a fact, having been her tutor, read her essays, heard her in discussion. She was extraordinary.'

'You sound as though you were in love with her yourself,' Susan said, reproachfully, or so it seemed to Paul, who reached for her hand as he said, 'There's no one to equal you, Mother dear.' It was half-playful, flirtatious even, but it assuaged her sense of momentary hurt.

Peter, catching the intention, the spirit of his son's words, said, 'And no one can equal your infinite variety, dear, sweet Sue.'

'Alright, alright,' she said, laughing, but shaking her head to dismiss the moment. 'Give over, the pair of you. Peter, call for the bill, please. I have a rehearsal later this afternoon.'

'But Paul hasn't yet given me an answer to my question. What am I supposed to do with DeVine's request?'

'Oh, that's easy,' Paul said. 'Arrange to see her, this Patricia, isn't she called?'

'She is,' Peter said.

'And who did the naming? Her father, the grandparents?'

'The grandparents, I should think,' Peter said. 'They were going to take care of her.'

'But they'd have told DeVine, surely. And I imagine he'd have gone along with it. Anyway, he was probably out of the picture by the time his child's christening took place.'

'Out of the picture as in "he couldn't care less?"'

'No,' Susan said to her husband, 'that's *not* what I meant. But he must have agreed to let them have the care of his daughter. After all, what choice did he have? He'd got no money, no way of caring for her, whereas they had plenty of both.'

'Well, anyway,' Paul said, 'I suggest you invite the young woman to come to your office, "where she may learn something to her advantage," as they used to say on the Beeb, or, better, propose that the two of you should meet for a coffee somewhere on campus. It shouldn't be difficult to explain to her that you taught her mother, that you know something of her sad story, are intrigued that her daughter should choose to enrol as a student at the same university ... what further excuse can you need for a social, fifteen-minute chat?'

'And if she says no?' Peter turned to gesture for the bill.

'She won't,' Paul told him. 'Why should she?'

Peter turned back. 'She might think *I'm* after her money.' He held up his hand. 'Sorry, that was a daft thing to say.'

He reached for his wallet as the bill was placed on a small tray before him, doled out some notes in a parody of a gaming club dealer. 'Marlon Brando,' he said as Paul smiled wonderingly at his father's gestures. '*Guys and Dolls*. The best musical ever.'

As they left the hotel, Paul said to Peter, 'I didn't have you down for a fan of musicals.'

'You wouldn't wonder if you heard him sing,' Susan said, taking her son's arm. 'Like a dying cow in its last agonies.'

'Jealousy,' Peter said, as the three of them strolled back to their house through the already dimming light of early November. 'Besides, Paul heard me sing often enough when he and Sally were small and I was putting them to bed.' Then momentarily wished he'd never spoken the words. There was too much of the past in them, that element open at each instant of our lives, as a great poet had written, linking us to our losses, showing us, in the words of a poem he knew by heart, *what we have as it once was, as if/By acting differently we could have kept it so.*

But the moment went. Paul was here, and in his presence his parents were happy.

That happiness, which Peter sensed all three of them shared, lasted through the afternoon while Susan was at rehearsal and father and son strolled through the city and down to the river embankment, pausing every so often to watch a few, late oarsmen sculling toward the nearby boat club, calling to each other through the thickening dusk; it enveloped them when they sat down to a leisurely supper arranged by both men, it wrapped them round during the evening's inconsequential chatter about the state of the University, the changes to the city since Paul had last paid his parents more than a fleeting visit, Susan's upcoming concert – 'I'll want to get to that,' Paul assured her, 'and I'll order Sally to bring Mark,' a man he told them, he'd come to like and trust from the few occasions they'd all met in London; and it persisted overnight, so that Sunday morning breakfast became a blessed time.

As they approached its end, Susan asked Paul whether he'd stay for tea. 'And before that we could go for a family walk.'

'I'd love to,' he said, 'but I need to get back. Go over my lines.' And he made a comic *moue*, a slightly camp intimation of taxing days ahead.

'Oh?' Susan was, suddenly alert, suspicious.

'Not lines for a play,' Paul said, laughing, 'I'm not thinking of strutting so much as a minute on the stage. No need to panic on that score.' He paused, said, as though inconsequentially, 'I'm thinking of applying for a new job. Social work, but out of London. I'm being interviewed tomorrow.'

'Where?'

'Where am I being interviewed?'

'Stop it,' Susan said, her face rigid with concern. 'You know what I mean. Where are you hoping – wanting – to find new work?'

'Africa,' Paul said. And quickly, to cut short Susan's wail of protest, he said, 'I loved that year of VSO I did when I'd finished at uni and before I went to London. It was a wonderful time, as I remember telling you both, and I've decided to return for a couple of years at least. I can be more use there than here.'

'Return to Nigeria?'

'Nigeria it is,' Paul said. And to Susan, who sat, mouth half open, aghast at his news, 'I know about the AIDS epidemic, Mother dear, of course I do, but you needn't worry. I've seen what it's done to several friends of mine in London and I'm not about to take any chances.'

Then, his voice deepening, he said, 'But someone's got to help.' He paused, looked down at his plate, then at both of his parents in turn. 'Fucking Thatcher,' he said, using a word he very rarely allowed himself with them. His voice was shaking with barely suppressed fury. 'We're stuck with what journalists call "the gay plague" and she tells everyone that homosexuality is not to be taught in schools. It only encourages vice, threatens to turn the dear little things against Christian purity.'

'Clause Twenty Eight,' Peter said.

Paul gave the merest of nods. 'So,' he said, when he could control his voice, 'I've decided to do what little I can to help. If all goes well at interview I'll be offered a two-year overseas contract and take up social work in Lagos or wherever I'm sent, wherever I can be most use.'

He leant back in his chair. 'So now you know,' he said.

'And I'm glad you told us.' Peter said. 'Very glad.'

An hour later Paul was ready to leave, but before he went to his car, he hugged them and kissed Susan on both her cheeks. 'I'll be in touch,' he said, 'I shan't be going before December at the earliest, I'm determined not to miss your concert, Mother dearest, and I'll let you have all the details of where exactly I expect to be posted after I've been given my orders in Lagos. Even in the Bush we'll be able to talk to each other on the telephone. We did when I was there last time, didn't we?'

A moment later, having thrown his overnight bag onto the back seat of his battered Honda, he was squeezed in behind the steering wheel.

'Good luck with the interview,' Susan felt impelled to call as Paul backed down the drive, and 'Drive carefully,' Peter said.

'I will,' their son shouted, waving from his open window, and then he was gone.

* * *

'I suppose they'll want him?' Susan said as the two of them stood clearing away the remains of their breakfast.

'Oh, he's already been accepted,' Peter said, his words, he knew, confirming her fears. 'He was breaking it to us as gently as he could. He knew you'd be worried.'

'Not you?'

'Of course, but it was you he was especially concerned for.'

There was silence between them until Peter said, 'Do you remember those three Americans we met in Orvieto? Three years ago last summer, when we did our train trek across Italy.'

Susan, momentarily puzzled, said, 'Remind me.'

But then, as Peter opened his mouth, she said, 'Oh, I remember.'

A further pause and now her look was troubled, sombre. 'Father, mother, and son. That's who you have in mind, isn't it? They were on a sight-seeing tour of Europe, taking in as many countries as possible before ... ' and she stopped.

'Before the parents left their son at some Greek monastery or other, yes.'

'Mount Athos,' Susan said. 'No need to remind me. A closed order, so they told us. Meaning that they might never see him again.' She looked enquiringly at Peter. 'That's who you have in mind, isn't it?'

He nodded without speaking.

'And he was their only child. And I remember that the woman called it God's Will. Poor woman, she looked so sad.

They all did, but especially her. Having to surrender the child she'd given birth to. And there they were, in their Sunday best, all dressed up to deliver the sacrificial lamb, you said.'

She shuddered. 'What an appalling religion.' Her voice was taut, vehement. She crossed to her husband, put her arms round his waist as she said, leaning back, her look challenging him, 'Well, we're not like that, are we.'

'We have a daughter.'

'Don't laugh at me,' Susan said, momentarily furious. 'You know what I mean.'

'I'm not laughing, promise,' he said, contrite, his lips brushing her hair. Hugging her, rocking their bodies from side to side, he said, 'Paul's off to Nigeria of his own free will, to do some good, and it's not a lifetime sentence. He'll be back in two years.'

'Let's hope so,' she said, but her voice was muffled and she wasn't, he knew, convinced.

10

BREAKFAST THE NEXT MORNING, MONDAY, WAS as always a hasty, stand-up-and-feed-yourself affair. Peter had to be up and out for a nine o'clock tutorial, and Susan was scheduled to take a practice session with the school choir. 'Handel,' she said, 'accompanied by a swelling chorus of yawns and groans as they drag themselves awake.' She reached for the cafetière. 'Medical authorities are always telling us that teenagers need more sleep. The ones at our school get quite enough – most of it in music class.'

She spoke breezily enough, but her strained attempt at a smile told him that she was still brooding over the news Paul had brought them, and he could think of nothing to say, apart from 'You'll soon have them chirping like nightingales.'

'Nightingales don't chirp,' Susan said, 'they trill. Don't you know the old rhyme – "Any twerp can chirp, But to trill takes skill."'

'You made that up,' Peter said. 'Be honest.'

'And you hurry up,' Susan said as she left the room. 'Your students will be waiting for you, anxious to know what they're supposed to think of – who is it this time?'

'Byron,' Peter said. 'His speech to the Lords about the Frame-Breakers Bill. Perfect for a Monday morning. Taking on the establishment.'

A few moments later he heard her call a farewell as she left the house and reminded himself to phone Sally, ask her to contact her mother.

He was in the act of opening his office door when he was hailed by a familiar voice. Simon Tims came limping along the corridor, a broad smile on his face, fist thrust aloft.

'Scored two on Saturday,' Tims said, reacting to Peter's pretend wince as he came alongside. 'No sympathy needed. But Carr Fasteners will be licking their wounds. We stuffed them.'

'And now you're going to tell me the score.'

'Four-nil,' Tims said, punching the air as he did so. 'Puts us in with a chance of promotion.'

'What to, the semi-geriatrics league?'

'Pathetic,' Tims said, grinning as he limped off. 'You should come and see us sometime. Do you good to watch the Academicals in action. All silky grace, that's us.'

Laughing obligingly, Peter went into his office, careful to prop his door ajar. New rule: 'Office doors are to be kept open when teaching is in progress.'

He glanced at his watch. Still time to try Jim Hobbs before any of his tutees appeared.

Might Professor Hobbs be at his post, he asked the secretary, and if so could Professor Randall have a word with him?

Yes and yes, he was told, and a moment later Jim Hobbs' voice came down the line loud and clear. 'Morning, Peter, and what can I do for you? State your business and show your working methods.'

'Patricia Connor, the first year student I mentioned the other day. I take it she's now back from her wanderings. If so, I'd like the chance to have a word with her, but not without clearance from her head of department.'

'You have it,' Jim said. 'But why should you need *my* permission?'

'Strictly speaking I probably don't, but if I put a foot wrong and she complains to you, you'll at least have advance knowledge of what I'm up to. Students are getting positively litigious these days. Not that I blame them, given the behaviour of some of our beloved colleagues, but I need to be cautious.' He paused. 'Anyway,' he said, 'she may not want to see me.'

'Point taken,' Jim Hobbs said, and rang off.

That evening, as he and Susan sat at the table, and worked their way through the mushroom omelette he'd prepared – 'Sorry there's little by way of salad,' he said apologetically – he waited to tell her about his phone call to Jim Hobbs. 'I asked him whether he'd mind my arranging to meet Patricia Connor, and he said of course not. So I've dropped her a line care of the Geography Department, explaining a little of why I'd like us to meet. Enough bait on the hook, I hope, to draw her in.'

Susan finished her omelette before, pushing aside her plate, she said, 'Sally phoned earlier, before you were home.' It was as though he had never spoken. Her mind was full of her daughter's conversation and of her important news.

'Oh?'

'She had to be quick. She and Mark are due at a performance of *Cymbeline*. But she wanted to ask whether we'd had a good weekend with Paul. Had he told us anything of interest?'

'So,' Peter said, 'she knows about Nigeria.'

'She does. Apparently he was full of it, told her he felt that from now on he ought to be known as The African Queen.

And he wants her and Mark to go out to see him as soon as he's settled in.'

'He didn't ask *us*,' Peter said, reaching to gather up his wife's plate.

Susan took his hand. 'He will,' she said, 'he will. I know he will.'

She met his gaze, smiled. 'We'd better start saving, air fares being what they are,' and he sensed her relieved gladness. Paul wasn't intending to cut himself free of his family. 'Now, tell me about your day,' she commanded.

'I already have,' Peter said.

'Then tell me again.'

So Peter, reasonably certain that Susan had no interest in hearing about Byron and the Luddites, repeated the story of his phone conversation with Jim Hobbs and, then, told her that he'd sent a note to the young woman, Patricia Connor.

'And what exactly did you say?'

'As little as possible. Told her that I'd taught her mother, knew about and was grieved by her tragic death, discovered by chance that she herself was now here, and wondered whether she'd care to meet for a coffee – on campus of course. Stressed that I had nothing but warm memories of her mother, and of her outstanding talent. Left it at that.'

'Sounds OK,' Susan said. 'Let's hope it works.'

It did. Two days later he found a note in his pigeon-hole telling him that Patricia Connor would be pleased to meet him and that she was usually free on Wednesday afternoons.

'How about next Wednesday?' he wrote back. '2pm in the Black Hole. I'll carry a copy of *The Guardian*. No need to reply if OK.' The Black Hole was a coffee bar favoured by arts students and a few members of staff, though he himself rarely went there.

The following Wednesday, feeling almost conspiratorial, he arrived at the bar – in truth more of a down-at-heel café with formica-topped tables and scuffed, black-upholstered chairs, most of the Rexine split or torn – found a table just about clear of used crockery and knives, deposited on it a mug of black coffee and, as he lowered himself gingerly onto a wooden stool across whose seat someone had scratched the legend *I'm all yours,* opened his newspaper and began to read.

He was still reading when, twenty minutes or so later, he became aware of someone standing at the other side of the table.

'Professor Simpson?'

He looked up, and as he did so almost cried out. Paddy Connor was staring down at him.

Slowly, he folded his newspaper, giving his heart time to cease its hammering, his breathing to return to normal. Nerving himself to look up once more, he accepted that it wasn't her. Of course it wasn't. This young woman was surely broader of face, and her questioning smile, though very like her mother's, was subtly different, less guarded, her lips fuller, the chin rounder. But this was his former student's daughter, without doubt.

As if to confirm his almost certainty, she said, 'I'm Patricia Connor.' Then, with the hint of the hesitant laugh he remembered so well, 'At your service.'

He cleared his throat, asked her to sit, wondered whether she would prefer coffee or tea, and watched, enthralled, as she shook her head. Ah, yes.

'I'm fine,' she said, 'no need of artificial stimulants.' And as she brought across a stool from an adjacent table and propped herself on it, she laughed again.

She was wearing a black leather jacket over her dark green T-shirt, and the black jeans encased, he sensed, slim legs.

'You taught my mother,' she said. It was as though she had said, 'Wonders never cease.'

'Yes,' he said, 'I taught your mother.' Then, feeling the

need to say more, he added, 'One of the best students I've known since I began teaching. She'd have got a first-class degree, no doubt about it.'

'When did you realise she was pregnant? *Did* you know?'

The abruptness of the questions startled him, sent him off balance. Slowly, giving himself time, he said, 'Yes, I knew, at least I think I did, though I'm not sure she told me in so many words.'

He paused, shook his head. 'I can remember that she introduced me to her partner – your father. We met one evening, by chance, in a local pub. November, probably, not long before the end of autumn term. I think that was soon after they'd ... after they'd come together, and following that meeting we sometimes coincided at The Swan, though I don't recall much more than an exchange of nods.' He was gabbling. 'It was obvious that they were deeply – deeply involved with one another.'

He hesitated, knew he should slow down, but couldn't. 'He wasn't a student.'

'Did my mother explain what my father did for a living? How he earned his money?'

Peter said, 'I think she must have told me he was some sort of a salesman.' And when she nodded, as though in confirmation, he added, 'That *did* surprise me, I suppose, though of course it was none of my business.'

He paused, drew breath. 'I was worried for her, I admit.'

'Why? Did you think he might be some sort of Sam-the-Seducer?'

He couldn't gauge her tone. Accusatory? Honestly enquiring? Did she have him down as some sort of class snob, a provincial moralist, wanting to keep far hence the wolf that preys on virgins?

Peter said, 'At first I worried she might be slackening off in her studies, but there was no need. Her written work was as good as ever, probably better.' His smile was intended to placate.

Then, speeding up, 'But when the spring term came to an end I began to suspect that something was amiss. I was, I know, surprised, that she never took her coat off even on the warmest days, and I fancied she was getting – well, plumper, if that's the right word. She told me, right at the end of term, the last time I saw her, that during the spring break she'd be going to Germany and taking her partner – I'm sure she called him that though she may have also referred to him as Terry – to meet her parents in Hamburg. I sensed she knew in advance that the meeting might be a sticky one, though how I sensed that I'm not really sure. Perhaps she pulled a face, or sighed. I can't remember.'

Peter stopped. 'Are you sure you wouldn't like a coffee? A glass of water, perhaps.'

But Patricia Connor shook her head. 'I'm fine as I am,' she said. 'But I'd like to hear whatever more it is you want to tell me.'

'OK. Well, I'll keep it short. I remember telling her, your mother, that I'd be delighted if she decided to take up the offer of the research scholarship the University could offer her. I'd already sounded her out about this and I know she was excited by it, but this time she was hesitant, said she couldn't yet give me a definite answer. I'd already sent a letter, as required, to her parents as next-of-kin, explaining that the English Department was hoping to offer their daughter the scholarship, subject to satisfactory performance in her final exams, of which I had no doubt.'

'Why did you need to do that?'

'Standard practice at the time,' Peter said. 'The scholarship would cover all expenses and a small honorarium beside. No need for them to dip into their own pockets. I'd no idea they were wealthy, nor need it have mattered, though I assumed they'd be pleased to learn that we thought so well of their daughter's academic achievements.'

'I've seen that letter,' Patricia Connor said.

'Really? How?' Peter was stopped in his tracks.

'Because,' Patricia Connor told him, 'my grandparents kept it in a bureau that was full of my mother's possessions. They let me rummage through, though they'd probably forgotten they'd put the letter in with her other belongings. I remember it almost word for word, especially the phrase "satisfactory performance".'

The young woman suddenly giggled. 'Like a seal, I thought. But I suppose they meant she'd need to get a first-class honours degree.'

'Not much doubt about that,' Peter said.

Patricia leant across the table. 'Do you know what my grandparents thought about the offer?'

'They'd have been pleased for her, I imagine,' Peter said. He drank his coffee. 'This is pure muck, by the way, you were wise not to ask for any.'

'They were furious. Livid, so my aunt told me. They wanted her to be a kind of society deb, until it was time for her to take up a top job in some international business or other, one her father would arrange. They had it all worked out. Once she'd got her degree her studying days would be over.'

She paused to study the effect of her words on Peter, before she resumed, 'And then she turns up pregnant, with a yob in tow, telling them that she plans to go on with university work, take up this scholarship, as soon as ever she can.'

Peter was stunned. 'But how can you know all this? I mean, you weren't – you hadn't been born.'

'Oh, they had plenty of time to tell me about this turn of events, this shocking revelation, through my childhood. Plenty of time, too, once I'd discovered the letter and asked about it, to explain to me the importance of not repeating my mother's mistake. They were not going to allow *me* to become involved with the wrong kind of man, as my grandmother put it. They blamed you, Professor Simpson, for turning her head, giving her – my mother – pipe dreams of becoming a "researcher".'

The young woman laughed. 'They made it sound the lowest of the low. And of course they blamed the University for making possible her involvement with the yob.'

Peter nodded. 'I heard that your grandfather wrote to the Vice Chancellor to complain. But to be honest I'm surprised they spoke so badly of DeVine to you. He was your father, for goodness' sake. He *is* your father.'

'As they never ceased to remind me.'

Had DeVine been a yob in those years, Peter wondered. To Paddy's own parents, he had, perhaps. He tried to remember what he himself had thought of the young man in his not especially well-fitting suit when Paddy had first introduced him some twenty years ago, but all he could recall was a youth, someone with a smile some would have regarded as ingratiating, a *professional* smile. The kind that went with being a hopeful man of business, just as his handshake had been, he supposed, intendedly firm, 'manly'.

But then there was that more recent meeting at The Swan, and DeVine's, 'Don't be so fucking condescending.' Well, the man had good reason to be angry, even if his words weren't those you might expect from someone announcing himself as a tax adviser. The street orphan showing through, perhaps.

Peter said, 'Did your grandparents tell you anything about your father – about his life, I mean?'

She shook her head. 'Nothing apart from his being brought up in an orphanage and trying to pass himself off as "something" better than he was. "Something" was her word, by the way. My grandmother's.'

She stopped, grimaced as she shook her head. 'I shouldn't really be talking about them in this way. They were snobs, still are, but in their way they were good to me. They took me in, looked after me, and, as my grandmother once told me, they gave up a good deal for my sake. Leaving the top job my grandfather had in Germany and returning to London so I could be sent to what they thought of as a good school. Oh, the sacrifice.'

The sceptical lift of an eyebrow left him in no doubt as to her own thoughts on the matter. How young she seemed, and at the same time how – assured, was that it? Very like her mother, that tilt of the head, the slightly oblique angle of gaze, at once cautious and yet determined.

He said nothing, and she took his silence as reason to continue. 'When my mother arrived, heavily pregnant, it seems they were about to begin packing in order to move to Freiburg. My grandfather had been offered a very senior post there and they were both excited at the chance to move to a city they liked – apparently they'd visited it in the late thirties – and which, they told me, had been spared the worst of the bombing. By the early 1960s the city and the surrounding Black Forest countryside looked, Gran said, as good as ever. But after their daughter's death they decided they'd have to return to England so I could have a "proper" education.'

'From all I've heard,' Peter said, 'you'd have had a good education in Germany.'

'But then I'd have grown up a Fraulein,' Patricia said, a smile flickering on her lips. 'Whereas now I'm a young English lady. I know the correct manner in which to hold a tea cup and how to ask the way to the toilet. Joke.'

A pause, before she added, 'And I had some very good teachers, some of whom remembered my mother and told me that she was one of their favourite pupils. I'm not sorry my grandparents sent me to that school.'

'What about your father, if you don't mind me asking. Didn't he have any say in the matter?'

She shrugged. 'I doubt it. I don't know, of course, because

they hardly ever mentioned his name, and when I came to know him he wouldn't talk about the past, beyond telling me that my mother was very beautiful and the love of his life. He said that often enough.'

A pause, 'Anyway,' she said, with a slight toss of the head, 'I never felt he wanted me to ask him about what had happened after my mother's death. I suppose he had very little money and I guess my grandparents wanted him out of my life. When I was old enough, about seven or eight, he was allowed to take me out for walks once or twice a month, but always a chaperone came with me. I took for granted that this strange man who came calling for me, and whom I always called Mr Terry even though I was told he was my father, would be an occasional visitor, and no more than that. There had been birthday and Christmas presents, with cards signed by "Your Daddy", but to be honest they didn't mean much to me. After all, I had plenty of presents, and I couldn't put a face to "Your Father," as my grandmother called him, with a kind of sniff. There were no photographs of him in the house – well, there wouldn't be, would there? And if it comes to that, the photographs I was shown of my mother were all of her before she went to university. I might as well have been found under a bush.'

She let out a short, slight laugh. 'Quite late on, when I was sixteen, at the time when my grandparents began to talk of moving to Spain, my grandmother told me of an incident that must have occurred much earlier, when I was young and the walks with my father had only recently begun. The chaperone let her know that on that particular Sunday's walk, "Mr Terry" said that perhaps when he'd earned enough money, he and I could set up house together, and wouldn't that be fun. I began to cry – I must have thought he was the Big Bad Wolf threatening to steal me away, and Miss Cherry, the chaperone, told my grandfather, I suppose.'

She met Peter's questioning gaze, before she spoke again.

'I imagine,' she said, speaking more emphatically, 'that was the occasion he sent for my father and told him he had no legal rights and that if he repeated such words I would be made a ward of court and that he'd be barred from ever seeing me. After that I didn't see my father for quite a long time, a year or so I think; and by the time he was allowed to visit once more, I was old enough not to fear him.'

Another laugh, this time rueful. 'Not much of a relationship for a father and daughter, is it?'

Quite suddenly, as though wanting to change the conversation, she asked, 'Do you have children?'

Peter nodded. 'One son, one daughter,' he said.

'And do you all get on well together?'

'Yes,' he said, 'as far as I know.' He was amused rather than offended by her presumption, and again aware of her self-confidence.

'Oh, good,' she said, her manner now off-hand as she stood to leave.

He too stood, and as though his movement was a signal, taped music from the bar burst into life, and a voice bawled some incomprehensible words above the thunder of guitar and drums.

'Noddy Holder,' Patricia shouted over the din. 'A bit retro, that.' She was laughing at Peter's anguished stare.

A moment later, as they stood in the open, the door to the café shut firmly behind them, Peter said, 'What would you like me to tell your father about our meeting? He'll be keen to know.'

He left it for a moment, and then, when she showed no sign of wanting to answer, said, 'Any message for him?'

She shrugged. 'I don't think so.'

But as she was about to turn away, she stopped, looked straight at Peter, and said, 'Would you mind if you and I met somewhere else for a coffee? I'd like to have the chance for more talk, but this place gives me the creeps.'

'Yes, I'd like that,' he said, 'then I could see you drink coffee,' laughing to hide his surprise at her unexpected question. He couldn't imagine what else they might have to say to each other, but she looked at once pleased and relieved. They left it that she would contact him sometime – leaving it vague – sometime before the end of term.

And with that, they went their separate ways.

But brooding over her words as he walked back to his office, it came to him that her suggestion of a further meeting was more spur-of-the-moment than considered request, and that by now she might well be regretting it. Apart from the knowledge they shared about her parents, and that was little enough, they had no reason to stay in touch. He had enjoyed their conversation, knew that he could truthfully offer DeVine a reassuring report on his daughter, on her academic abilities and on her social self-confidence, but what more was there to say that couldn't as well or better be said by others? The young woman was in no need of Peter's help. If she contacted him then of course he'd be happy to meet her again. But he doubted she would. And thinking that, he felt both relieved and content. With her, with himself, and, it came to him, content also for DeVine. DeVine had a good daughter.

11

'YOU JUST MISSED YOUR DAUGHTER,' SUSAN said, as Peter came into the kitchen.

'Sally phoned? She's earlier than usual.'

'You're later than usual.'

Peter crossed to where Susan stood over the stove, stirring the contents of a saucepan. 'Main course soup,' she said. 'Otherwise known as leftovers from the weekend.'

He kissed the nape of her neck, put his arms round her waist and said, 'I was delayed at Uni by one of my least favourite students, who thought he should tell me that he considered my views on Coleridge misguided. STC's problem was, I needed to be informed, psychological insecurity. He was basically an intuitive introvert masquerading as an aggressive extrovert.'

He opened the fridge and took out a bottle of white wine. When he straightened up he saw that Susan had turned from her culinary duties and was staring at him, a sceptical smile on her face. 'Pull the other one,' she said.

'No,' Peter said, 'word of truth swelp me god.' He held the bottle out to her enquiringly. 'Fancy a glass?'

She shook her head. 'Not till I've put our food on the table.'

'Cadwell – the student in question – told me it's all in Jung,' Peter said, taking a mouthful of wine. 'Ah, that's better.'

'I didn't think anyone read Jung nowadays,' Susan said.

'Cadwell does.'

'And what did you tell him. That he was too Jung for such writing.'

'Ha, bloody ha. No, I suggested, very politely, that Coleridge's poetry was far too complex to be "explained" away as though he was some sort of a nutcase, though I'd try to keep Cadwell's comment in mind.'

'And what did he say to that?' Susan ladled out two large bowls of the soup and brought them to the kitchen table.

Peter picked up a soup spoon and took an experimental mouthful. 'Delicious,' he said, as he reached for a hunk of bread. 'He said he was pleased to be of use.' He tore off some bread, dipped it in his soup.

'Now,' he said, pouring some wine into Susan's glass, 'tell me what Sally had to say.'

'She wanted to talk about Paul. Had he told us anything about his future plans? She knew he'd been up at the weekend, assumed he'd want to keep us informed, and was wondering about our reaction.'

'So Paul's taken her into his confidence?' Peter felt a twinge of – what, envy, hurt?

'They've always been close, my love,' Susan said. 'I've no doubt Sally knew about his sexual preferences some time before he came out to us.'

Peter nodded. 'I expect she did,' he said, but the pang was still there. We think we know our children, but of course there's so much in their lives we can never share.

He shut the thought away. Susan was speaking again. 'Sally thinks he's not at all sure about the African venture. He may have been hoping we'd try to dissuade him. She told me that on previous occasions he's said to her that he felt he ought to go somewhere overseas to find what it is he really wants to do with his life.'

She looked at her husband, smiling wistfully. 'He sees us as two people who were certain of our careers from the start.'

'Blimey,' Peter said, 'and did you tell our beloved daughter that it wasn't like that at all.'

'I did. I reminded her that you only avoided National Service by the skin of your teeth and that you'd planned to bunk off – go to Canada – if the army came for you.'

'And that you weren't at all sure you'd come with me.'

Susan finished her soup before, laying down her spoon, she looked levelly at Peter. 'I reminded her that when I was the age she is now I'd been wanting to spend some time in France, studying music, that I'd been offered a year's scholarship at Lyons, but then of course my mother became very ill and I had to stay to help my father ... '

'And I got deferment from National Service because I'd landed a research studentship ... '

Peter pushed his empty bowl aside. 'And then that assistant lectureship came up and between us we had just enough money to marry and live in a shoe-box flat with more water running down the walls than ever came out of the taps ... '

'And the rest, allowing for some bends and bumps in the road, is history,' Susan said. 'The quirks of chance. But isn't it strange, your own children think that their parents' lives were all planned out from day one.'

She stood. 'Nostalgia, as I read somewhere, means sickness of the soul. Face forward, press on, confront the unknown, and all those other Speech Day clichés. Would you like a refill, or should we move on to the cheese course?'

'Cheese,' Peter said. 'I have a sudden, uncontrollable, anti-nostalgic desire for a thick slice of cheddar.' He too stood and carried their bowls over to the sink.

As they settled again into their chairs, he said as he stared unseeing at the block of cheese Susan had placed between them, 'But I know how much you regretted missing out on that year in France.'

'The year I'd so looked forward to,' Susan said. 'If I'd gone to Lyons everything might have been different.' She looked at him. Then away. 'Not that the children knew about that.'

'You never even mentioned it to either of them?'

In the act of raising the cheese knife, Peter stopped, uneasy, a feeling of obscure guilt – was it? – troubling him. He wanted to say, 'It couldn't be helped, could it, neither of us could have guessed that you'd become pregnant, not then, not so soon after our marriage began.'

But it was easier not to utter the words. Instead, he said, 'Well, I suppose from the outside it must seem that we're Mr and Mrs Average.' And was relieved when Susan said, 'You're not *that* average, mi duck,' so that he could reply, 'And neither are you, Mother, not by a long chalk.'

'A long chalk? What on earth does that mean?'

'It's a chalk you use to reach out and mark a special person. You'll find it in Partridge. "Low. Coll. Nineteenth Century."'

Susan laughed. 'If it's in Partridge he'll almost certainly add "male member". And he won't mean a gentleman's club.'

'Oh, I don't know,' Peter said, 'it depends how you interpret the word "club".' They both laughed, good humour restored. 'Still,' he said, 'I'm sorry, very sorry, that Paul is so undecided about his future.'

'He's young,' Susan said. 'He doesn't need to be certain of the way ahead. He's talented, he'll find out what he wants to do soon enough.'

But he could tell that she was less confident than her words suggested.

'And now,' she said, 'tell me about your day, Cadwell apart, that is.'

'Shall I make coffee first?'

She nodded. 'Good idea. Although I'd prefer you to wash up while I labour over the coffee. Fair dobs?'

They looked at each other and both of them laughed. "Fair dobs."

It was an expression Paul had picked up at Cubs when he was a small boy and which from time to time the whole family used. 'Yes,' Peter agreed, 'fair dobs.'

* * *

'So,' Susan said, as some half-an-hour later they once more sat facing each other across the kitchen table, 'your day. I want to hear about your meeting with DeVine's daughter.'

Peter was momentarily startled by the words. 'It sounds odd when you put it that way. "DeVine's daughter". I've not thought of her like that. Still,' he said, 'I suppose it's no more than the truth.'

He drank his coffee, cradled the empty cup between his two hands. 'But I can tell you, I was pretty shaken when she turned up in the coffee bar. For a moment I could have sworn I was looking at her mother.'

'The resemblance was that close? Not a scrap of DeVine about her?'

Peter shook his head. 'I don't think so. Not a hint. As far as I can remember, this was Paddy Connor to the life.'

'I can imagine that would have been – well – upsetting, I suppose.'

And as Peter nodded, Susan asked him, 'And what did you make of her?'

'Self-assured, like her mother. But then she'd been to the same school, one where they no doubt teach self-assurance as part of the syllabus. "Today we have How to Look Your – sorry, One's – Interlocutor Straight in the Eye". That kind of thing.'

Susan's own look was sceptical. 'You make her sound pretty well insufferable.'

'I don't mean to,' Peter said. 'Considering all she's been through, she seemed fine. Level-headed, articulate – no, that's making her sound like the object of a written reference. "Miss Connor is remarkably mature for her age and I recommend her unhesitatingly for the post of gym instructor." But she's no Orphan Annie.'

He grimaced. 'No, I don't mean that, either. I mean, at least I think I mean, that if I were DeVine I'd see no reason to worry about her. She must have had a difficult start to her life but as far as I can tell from our brief encounter, she's turned out ok. Like him, she's learned to be pretty well self-contained. But then they're both as good as orphans. They've learned to do without mother love.'

'And that's what you'll tell him? Tell DeVine?'

'I guess so, though that probably won't satisfy him.' He stopped, then said, 'And if I was in his place it probably wouldn't satisfy me, either. After all, she's his daughter and he'd like them to be better than virtual strangers. Remember how anxious we both were when Sally went off to Manchester. Away from home for the first time, having to fend for herself, our lovely daughter, certain to be preyed on by randy males. I know it's a rite of passage, leaving home for pastures new, I know how capable Sally seemed ... '

Susan said, 'And I suppose DeVine would be bound to remember the harm he'd done to one of your star students.'

Staring into his cup, Peter said, 'Ironic, of course. DeVine is probably worried about his daughter meeting and falling for the kind of man her own father was. Please spare her from that fate, Professor Simpson.'

'And make sure her money stays locked away in her bank account?'

'I don't really believe any of that,' Peter said. He shook his head emphatically. 'She – Patricia – wanted me to be in no doubt that in her early years her grandparents were genuinely devoted to her.'

'But from all you tell me they wanted her to be a replica of her mother – pre-DeVine, that is. They took as many precautions as they could to keep him away from her, didn't they?'

Peter shrugged. 'Yes, I suppose they did. But then he had precious few rights. They had the law on their side. He and Paddy weren't married, they weren't even engaged.'

'They were ships that passed in the night,' Susan said, her smile sceptical. 'Except for the little matter of a child in the offing.'

But Peter, pursuing his own line of thought, wasn't listening. 'When the two of them came to see me, not long before they went to Germany to tell her parents, Paddy asked me whether her place could be left open for her to take up again the following year. She explained that they both wanted her to complete her degree and that, once the baby was born and she could get back to her studies, they'd find a way to share domestic responsibilities. She was *very* keen to let me know that they didn't want to be beholden to her parents. "I'm not prepared to have them boss me about," she said. "They'll want to make me 'a respectable woman' of course. Insist on an engagement ring, hurry me to the altar. But I won't do it."

'I remember glancing at DeVine while she said all this, and he was gazing at her in a kind of wonder of admiration. There's no doubt that he was besotted with her. Although that's the wrong word. "Committed", that might be better. Utterly committed.'

Susan was looking – was it disbelievingly – at her husband.

'Hold hard,' she said. 'You've never told me this before. All I knew was that a favourite student of yours had suddenly disappeared from view, and that you later found out she'd been pregnant at the time of her disappearance. Oh, and that the father was a dodgy customer you didn't trust.'

'Is that right?'

'Yes,' Susan said, 'that's right.'

'I must have been trying to spare you more than I thought you'd want to know.'

'Really?'

'Yes,' Peter said, 'really. You could get edgy – more than that – if I "maundered on" as you put it, about students, when you were here burdened with small children who were *your* responsibility. Hint, hint. They should have been mine too. Well, they were, at all events I always thought they were. Still,' he added, 'I guess I did get caught up, more than I'd intended, in "pastoral care" for students.'

'And her in particular.'

Peter looked at his wife, then away. 'Sorry,' he said.

Susan accepted his apology with a small smile, and quick nod of the head. 'Ah, well,' she said, 'it was a long time ago, and we're still together.'

'More than that,' he said. 'Far more than that.'

After a lengthy pause in which, meeting each other's eyes, they acknowledged that silent acceptance was better than speech, Susan said, 'Of course abortion wasn't on the cards. Not then. Not legal abortion, anyway.'

'They'd never have considered it,' Peter said, shocked by his wife's words.

Into the ensuing silence, Susan said, murmured rather, 'A true child of the Sixties.'

Peter said, 'How much *did* I tell you? I can't remember. I did, I know, tell you that one of my best students was having to leave the University because she was pregnant, but I've no recollection of saying much more than that.'

'Well, you did. And I felt envious of them. Not about the girl's condition, of course, I wouldn't have fancied that, but being free of constraints, able to choose your life ... '

'They weren't free,' Peter said. He was suddenly, obscurely, unnerved by Susan's words. 'They'd very little money, they'd have to find somewhere to live, DeVine would need to be out most of the time hustling for work, and Paddy would be stuck in cramped quarters, looking after the baby. I wouldn't call *that* freedom.'

'No need to raise your voice,' Susan said. 'Besides, what you say about your student wasn't that much different from my condition at that time, was it? Stuck in a flat with *two* small children while *you* swanned off to the University and spent your day surrounded by nubile eighteen-year-olds, each of them gazing up at you adoringly and hoping they'd be the one you'd take to bed.'

'Now you're raising *your* voice,' Peter said. After a moment, he said, 'And anyway, we were soon able to buy a house, remember, and you could go back to being a music teacher.'

There was a further silence. Then Susan said, smiling, a small, rueful smile, 'Well, we're still together.'

'And I never fancied anyone but you,' Peter said.

'Not even Paddy Connor?'

'She had a partner,' Peter said. 'And no, I didn't fancy her. Her death was horrible, but what I mourned was the loss of so much promise.'

Even as he spoke them, his words, he realised, sounded both defensive and pompous, so he added, 'Perhaps her daughter can make up for that loss.'

Which wasn't much better.

Susan said, 'And what does your friend, Jim Hobbs, think are the chances of that?'

'Jim doesn't teach her,' Peter said. 'He certainly doesn't know much, if anything, about Patricia Connor, and I'm not going to tell him more than I have to.'

More silence, then Susan got up, crossed to Peter, and, leaning down, kissed him full on the lips, before, looking into his eyes, she said, 'And make sure, my love, that after you've told DeVine you've met his daughter and you can report that she's happy and well, you keep clear.'

'I'll try,' Peter said. 'But she asked if she could see me again.'

Straightening up, Susan said, 'And I hope you told her that you don't think there's any need for that.'

Meeting her gaze, Peter, holding his upturned hands out to her in a gesture of hapless supplication, said, 'I told her I would.'

'Oh for god's sake,' his wife said, exasperated. 'You don't owe the man any more, and nor do you owe her a thing. Let it go, why don't you?'

'Because,' Peter said, 'as I was about to leave – I had a lecture to give and I was in a rush – she told me that there's something she'd been very much wanting to tell me. Something of importance, that is.'

Susan said, 'She probably thinks you're a soft touch, a kind of rich uncle.' The asperity in her voice was unmistakable. 'This time a coffee, next time a three-course dinner.'

'No,' Peter said, 'she meant it, I'm sure. And I want to hear what she has to say.'

12

THE FOLLOWING DAYS WERE TAKEN UP with work routines. Lectures on the English Romantics which with luck Peter would be able to incorporate into the *Short History of English Poetry* he'd promised to deliver to his publisher by the end of the academic year, tutorials, which he invariably enjoyed, and attendance at a couple of open guest lectures, one on the possible authorship of 'Pearl', given by a woman with whom he had himself been a student and who was now a distinguished mediaevalist teaching at a Scottish university. Her poorly attended lecture was, as he told her over dinner afterward, excellent, and he took pleasure in her recognition of his genuine appreciation of her talk.

The other lecture was given by a young man who wore jeans and an expensive-looking black leather jacket beneath which his T-shirt proclaimed *We Will Rock You.* His subject was 'Deconstructing the Pronoun: the Turn of the Hypallagic', and his talk attracted a large crowd, most of whom nodded gravely or smiled knowingly or listened with their eyes shut, and some of whom used the question time that followed the speaker's warmly applauded talk to express reservations about the possible totalising implications of his position, or who would wish to argue that one could hypothesise fruitful, not to say enabling, variations on his thesis.

'Hypothesise the hypallagic,' Simon Tims murmured, who was sitting next to Peter, 'well, it beats staff meetings.'

Earlier that afternoon the pair of them had spent two hours in one such meeting, during which tempers became frayed over the all-important subject of who was allowed to have open access to the stationery cupboard, a matter which caused some members of staff to 'happen to think' something or the other, while others maintained a 'studious neutrality' even when the question was put to the vote. (Ten in favour of open access, two opposed, 'as a matter of integrity', the two being the Head of Department and his secretary, five abstentions.)

As he walked away from the lecture hall and made for the car park, Peter was hailed by Jim Hobbs.

'Slipped in late,' Jim said, 'had to sit at the back, among the sleepers.'

'Did you enjoy the talk?' Peter asked him.

'Didn't understand a word of it,' Hobbs said. 'Is that what your lot regularly get up to when you're left alone with defenceless students? A lecture like that should come with a Government Health Warning. "This Could Seriously Affect Your Sleep Patterns."'

Peter laughed. 'Any more of that and I'll send him to bite your cultural geographers. That'll larn 'em.'

'You leave the poor lambs alone,' Hobbs said. Then, as they came to the car park, he said, 'Fancy a drink? Wash away any remaining traces of hypallagy.'

Peter shook his head. 'I'd love to, but I promised Susan that I'd be home at an early hour so she can have the car. She's deep in rehearsals for the Christmas concert.'

'The Clifton Quintet? Haven't they rehearsed enough by now?'

'They've managed to obtain the services of a big-name guest violinist,' Peter said, 'so I'm told. I gather tickets are nearly all gone, and they're anxious to be on top form.'

'Clarrie's already bought ours,' Hobbs said, confirming an earlier promise of attendance, 'we'll be there, alright. In the front row. But we *must* meet up for a proper meal, sometime soon.' Then, in the act of turning away, he asked, 'Have you met your Miss Connor as yet?' And when Peter nodded, he added, 'And what's the verdict?'

'She seems as assured as any nineteen-year-old I've come across,' Peter said. 'Well-adjusted, is that the phrase? When I meet her father I'll be able to tell him there's nothing to worry about, and that I suggest he leaves well alone. I don't think she's all that keen to meet – see him, anyway.' He decided not to mention that Patricia had asked Peter himself for another meeting.

* * *

By the time he got back to the house Susan was already dressed to go out, her cello propped up beside the front door. Picking it up, she asked, 'Did you remember to leave the car in the road?'

'And there's a full tank of petrol,' he said. 'I filled up on the way home.'

'Thanks.' But there was no warmth in her rushed acknowledgement as she picked up her instrument before opening and slamming the door shut in her haste to be gone.

'Drive safely,' he said, to the closed door. He glanced at his watch. Even with his detour to the filling station he was back, as they'd agreed he would be, before seven.

He went through to the kitchen, glanced at the table and

saw the note she'd left. *No time to make food. 5.45 pm. DeVine phoned.*

Underneath that there was a further note. *6.10 pm. P Connor phoned! Wanted to speak to you!!!*

Puzzled and made uneasy by her curt manner, he went to the fridge, took out an opened bottle of Chablis and a hunk of cheese, spread butter on two slices of bread and, without bothering to sit down, chewed his sandwich as he looked again at Susan's scrawled notes. Then he took the wine bottle and a glass into his study and sat at his desk, typing up some notes on John Clare, a favourite poet and someone who, when he'd first begun to lecture on him some twenty years ago, very few mentioned, though Clare was becoming a kind of hero to many, the young especially.

Three hours later, while he was still typing out his account of Clare's *Village Minstrel,* he heard the key turn in the front door, then the sound of Susan's feet along the hall floor, followed by the running of tap water and its drumming as she presumably filled the kettle for a cup of late evening tea.

He waited for a few minutes, then, pushing away his Olivetti, got up from his desk and went out to join his wife.

She was standing at the sink, her back to him, still in her outdoor coat as she waited for the water to boil.

He went across to her, put his hands on her shoulders and said as he kissed the nape of her neck, 'No point in watching the kettle. It'll never boil, you know.'

She did not turn to him, said, her voice taut with what had to be anger, 'Did you see the note your secretary left for you?'

'My secretary?'

She swung round, stared at him, her eyes hard, unblinking. 'Yes, ME, your bloody secretary.'

He looked back, bewildered now, unsure. 'What's brought this on?'

Steam was huffing from the kettle's spout. 'Shall I make you tea?' he asked.

For answer she crossed to the kitchen table, saying as she went, 'Oh, certainly, oh, please do, a cup of tea will make everything right.'

Peter filled the pot, poured for them both, took the mugs over to where his wife now sat, refusing to meet his eyes, and, as he joined her at the table, said, 'Wouldn't you like to take your coat off?'

'Don't Tell *Me* What To *Do*.'

'I wasn't telling you, I didn't mean ... '

'Oh, shut up.' She folded her arms, bent forward until her head was sheltering in her coat sleeves, and burst into tears.

They sat in silence for some minutes before, raising her head, she looked momentarily at him, her eyes bleary from weeping as she uttered a single word before once more lowering her face to the shelter of her arms.

What was it? Paul? Sally? Had something dreadful happened to either of the children? Bereft of words, he fixed his eyes on her averted head, the few spidery threads of grey among her shoulder-length hair, then, tentatively, reached out to place a hand over one of hers.

'Sorry,' she muttered.

'Susan, what's wrong?'

She lifted her face. 'I'd better go to bed,' she said.

'Why not drink your tea first?'

'Yes, nurse.'

But there was the hint of a smile as she raised the mug to her lips and emptied its contents in a series of prolonged gulps.

'Now can I go to bed?'

'I'd rather you'd tell me what's wrong.' He was pleading with her. 'Have you heard anything from London, from one of the kids – from either Paul or Sally?' Though if it was that she'd surely have left a note, or more likely cancelled her practice session.

'They're not "kids", you know that,' she said. 'But no, it's nothing to do with them.'

Relief flooded through him, as strong as ever it had been when one of the children came weeping from junior school over a broken friendship or, in their adolescent years, mourned in incommunicable sadness for an unfavourable teacher assessment or slow exclusion from a group of classmates.

He shifted in his chair, wanting to reach out for Susan, put his arms round her, but as though to prevent this she now stood, gathered up both their mugs and took them over to the sink.

From the safety of distance, she said, 'I don't do *anything* as well as I want to. Most days my teaching is ... is no better than average, and I can see most of them looking at their watches, wanting the class to be over. And my cello playing is mostly a struggle to master the score, and I'm never asked to perform a solo. Never. This evening, before you got back, I had a call from Smarmy Smart, asking me whether I'd mind "awfully" if Charles Deare took my chair for the Bach we're rehearsing. "I *do* think he's a better fit for it, if you know what I mean. Charles brings something rather special to his bowing, as I'm sure you'll agree."'

'Smarmy Smart? He's the leader isn't he?'

Susan nodded.

'And *did* you agree? Or did you tell him to tie a brick round his neck and jump into the river?'

'I agreed,' Susan said. 'He's right. But you can imagine how it feels, can't you, to turn up for practice knowing that the others all think you're a failure?'

She banged her fist down on the draining board. 'And meanwhile I have to take messages for you, for my husband, Big Shot Simpson.' Her anger was building again.

Peter said, 'Susan, shut up.'

He got up from his chair, and a moment later was enclosing her in his arms.

For a further moment she struggled against his grip, then went limp.

'If you're a failure then explain why the Elgar's been chosen for the climax of the concert *precisely* to exhibit your talent. Your name's on the posters, isn't it. This Deare is being given a chance to show *his* talent, that's all. And as for some pupils not wanting to attend music class, what's new? When I was at school we ran through music teachers quicker than D'Artagnan skewered his enemies. And don't ask me where I got that from because I can't remember. But I *can* remember the poor sods whose lives we made a misery by the way we treated them in Music Appreciation. That's what those classes were called. Licensed mayhem was nearer the mark. Lessons in who could fart loudest or ask the stupidest question. "This Vorgan Williams, Sir. Is he the one who played centre-half for Brentford?"; "Sir, am I right in thinking a cantata is a tin of potatoes?" Most of them had nervous breakdowns, the rest went off to live the free and easy life of a street busker.'

'Liar,' Susan said.

'No, I'm not. We used to see one of them up in London. Playing the accordion while he did a soft-shoe shuffle. Reckoned it was a doddle after trying to get us to approve the finer points of Beethoven.'

As she laughed, reluctantly, Peter said, 'And as for those phone calls, if, as I suspect, they caught you on the raw, they're no big deal. DeVine is hoping I'll report back to him on my meeting with his daughter, and *she* – well, I don't know what she wants of me although it won't be to offer me a lucrative book contract or an invitation to give a BBC series of talks on "What You Always Wanted to Know About How Romantic Poets Wore Their Trousers."'

'I didn't think Romantic poets wore any trousers.'

'They most certainly did,' Peter said. 'Open, closed, and half-mast. Or in Byron's case, full mast.'

Some minutes later, upstairs now and undressing for bed, Susan said, 'Thanks, love, for lifting my mood.' Her smile was uncertain, then defiant. 'Though you may well have to put up with further outbursts, or worse.' She sat for some minutes in silence on the edge of their bed. 'I don't really mind about Charles Deare,' she said. 'He's a good musician.'

'And so are you,' Peter said. 'You know you are.'

Susan turned her head to him, her smile half grateful, half abashed, then looked away as she raised her arms for him, as always, to drop her nightdress over her head. Her voice muffled by the descending cascade of satin, she asked, 'Have you noticed what the shrinks call "mood swings" in me, recently?'

And when he looked enquiringly at her emerging face, she said, enigmatically as it seemed to him, 'Time of life.'

'I love you,' he said, as he climbed into bed and turned to face her. 'For better or for worse.'

He rested a hand on her stomach.

'That helps,' she said.

13

DEVINE PHONED PETER THE NEXT MORNING, contacting him at the University. 'Sorry about last night,' he said. 'I thought you'd be in, but your wife told me you weren't expected back for a further half hour. So I thought I'd better leave it.' He paused. 'She seemed a bit short with me.'

'Susan was due at rehearsal,' Peter said.

'Oh, yeh. She's a musician, isn't she? I remember Paddy told me about that. Plays violin.'

'Cello,' Peter said. 'Now, how can I help you?'

'Blimey,' DeVine said. 'Everything alright, is it? You sound as though you got out of bed the wrong side.'

'I've a tutorial in a few minutes,' Peter said.

'OK. I'll make this snappy. Any chance we can meet on Friday – for lunch? I'll be on my way to Hull.'

'If it's early,' Peter told him. 'Eleven-thirty at The Swan do you? I'll need to be away by one o'clock.'

'Eleven-thirty it is,' DeVine said, and rang off.

Damn, damn, damn. Peter had no great wish to see DeVine again. This, he promised himself, would have to be the last time. He'd tell the man that he'd done his duty, met Patricia

Connor for a coffee, and that as far as he could tell she was a self-assured young woman, quite capable of looking after herself. He wouldn't mention that she claimed to have an 'urgent' reason for wanting to see him again. He had absolutely no wish to give DeVine any cause for requesting further contact. DeVine's early years and the horror of his lover's death were cause for sympathy, right enough, but he was now a successful man of business, and surely not someone who qualified for continuing attention. When it came to the point, Peter told himself, he didn't even like him. There was still something pushy about him, a kind of implicit desire to claim an emotional connection to Peter that Peter instinctively resisted, distrusted even. He'd have to tell DeVine that he wanted out. He'd done what he'd been asked to do, established, as far as he could, that Patricia was fine, that she obviously knew her own mind in signing up to be a student in the University, and that he really didn't see himself in the role of hired private detective. Nor did he intend to. Finito.

He was about to welcome in his tutorial group when once more his phone rang.
'Patricia Connor,' the voice said. Could they meet again *soon* because she wanted to tell him something she thought he ought to know. Reluctantly he said yes, and suggested Thursday afternoon, an off-campus coffee bar he sometimes used where the coffee was reliably decent, told her how to find it, they agreed on five o'clock, 'Clocking-off time from classes,' she said, and put the phone down before he could think of a reply.

* * *

They met at the appointed time and place. Was it his imagination, or did she look rather more nervous – apprehensive – than at their first meeting?

'I really can't be long,' he said, fearing that her apparent need for urgent disclosure might be little more than an excuse for further conversation with a university professor, a forlorn attempt to impress her contemporaries.

But what she had to tell him forced him to say, 'I'm meeting your father tomorrow morning, I'll have to discuss this with him.'

'Please yourself,' she said, and they left it at that.

* * *

'Too early for me to risk alcohol,' DeVine said, as, the next morning, the two men stood at the saloon bar of The Swan waiting for the landlord to appear. 'I've a longish car journey ahead of me. But can I get you something. Beer? Wine?'

'Coffee will be fine,' Peter said.

At this hour of the day The Swan's saloon bar was empty apart from one table where a small group of middle-aged women sat grouped in intense conversation. Watching the two men carry their cups to a table well away from them, one of the women rose, came across, and handed them a leaflet each. GREENHAM WOMEN'S SUPPORT GROUP, the leaflet was headed. 'Any help welcome,' she said, holding out a collection tin, 'garments, money offerings.'

'You won't get many pairs of jeans in there, love,' DeVine said, handing the woman a ten pound note and grinning. Peter reached into his jacket, fished out a fiver from his wallet, and gave it to her. 'Good luck,' he said. She thanked them both and went back to where the other women sat, watching, and then, as she reported her success, they smiled approvingly in the men's direction. 'We shall overcome,' one of them called out, as they went back to their discussion.

'Is your wife involved in this malarkey?' DeVine asked Peter.

'She and our daughter were there for a weekend,' Peter

said. 'But now that the Americans are installing their missiles ... '

'Courtesy of Tarzan in his flak jacket.'

Peter laughed briefly. 'Yes, Hezza the hero.' Then, 'I had a coffee with your daughter – with Patricia – yesterday afternoon,' he said.

'Oh, yes?' DeVine had become suddenly cautious, shoulders straightened. He was watching Peter closely, not about to say more, wanting Peter to make the running.

'She told me there were some ... some unresolved questions about the nature of her mother's death she thought I should know about, especially if I planned on seeing you again. She seemed – bothered, upset, though she couldn't, or anyway wouldn't, tell me much more than that.'

DeVine lifted his cup, but without tasting the coffee, returned the cup to its saucer, his fingers tight round the yellow rim. But he said nothing.

Peter said, 'I've been wondering whether you know what the questions are likely to be, and why they trouble your daughter?'

'I wasn't there when Paddy died,' DeVine said. He looked at Peter, then away, then dropped his head so that his next words were difficult to make out.

'Sorry,' Peter said, 'I can't hear what you're saying.'

DeVine's head jerked up, his eyes now fixed on Peter's. 'I said, *or* when she was killed. That's what I said.'

His eyes were now fixed on Peter's. He took a deep breath, said, 'It was her aunt told my daughter, and my daughter told me. If you want to know, I don't believe it, not in the way it's been put, but that old biddy was sure of it. Or anyway, she was sure her niece ought to be told.'

Peter said, 'Patricia didn't want to say much, I think she found it too upsetting. But she thinks you know all about it, not so much from what *she* told you, but what others did, or may have known, and that you'll be prepared to tell me.'

'And why would I do that?'

'No idea,' Peter said. 'Perhaps because it's better out than in. And also because if I'm trying to help you, I deserve to be told whatever there is to know.'

He looked at DeVine's bowed head and as he did so the other man suddenly straightened up and met his gaze.

'Alright,' DeVine said, 'I'll tell you. How long have you got?'

Peter drank his coffee in two quick swallows, and glanced at his watch. 'An hour,' he said, 'then I need to be back in my office. I'm meeting a research student.'

'An hour,' DeVine said. 'That should be long enough.' He took a deep breath. 'Here goes,' he said.

Walking hastily back to campus rather more than an hour later, Peter wondered what to make of DeVine's story. He'd need to talk it over with Susan. There was more to tell, DeVine had said, but that could wait until he and Peter were able to meet again, perhaps the far side of the weekend, on Monday, when he'd be returning from Hull. Would Peter be free that lunchtime? Yes, Peter would be free. And for the moment, he told himself, he'd do better to shut DeVine's revelations away from the forefront of his mind: he needed to be clear-headed when he and Mary Hastings discussed her most recent chapter of the thesis she was working on, about Anglo-Indian fiction in the nineteenth century, a thesis he had no doubt would become a published work. That, at least, was pretty well beyond doubt.

He was a few minutes late arriving at his office and Mary was already standing outside his door, pretending an interest in the notices pinned to it.

'A busy man,' she said with a forgiving smile, as he half ran along the corridor toward her, then, short of breath, stood aside to let her enter.

'Sorry,' he said, 'you've not been waiting long, I hope.'

Sinking into the chair she usually occupied, Mary smiled. 'How do you think I came by all this grey hair,' she said.

He went round to his side of the desk, explaining that he'd been lunching with a man he'd known for years. 'The love of his life was a student of mine, she died in childbirth.'

Mary opened her mouth and to prevent her from having to utter some conventional expression of regret, he added, 'He's a loner, grew up in an orphanage.'

Which made matters worse, and as soon as he'd spoken he wished he'd kept silent. His words made him sound as if he himself was in need of sympathetic understanding. Forgive my lateness, I was offering the poor man a measure of my own generosity of soul. Though in truth the previous hour with DeVine had been pretty unsettling.

Mary shrugged. 'That's not so uncommon,' she said, 'not so uncommon as you might think. Quite a few people have died young, you know, war, disease, poverty... My own mother grew up in an orphanage.' A look of sadness, of introspection, crossed her face, and then was gone. 'But she was a lovely mother to me. And she loved having grandchildren.'

She was looking down at her hands as they grasped the notes she'd brought with her. 'I've read that children who grow up in an orphanage always carry the scars. But my mother wasn't cold or indifferent. All through my childhood she was very, very good to me, and to my siblings, she and my father took us on holidays, encouraged us to have friends, bring them home for tea, play games ... I had a wonderfully happy childhood, we all did. That old phrase, "A child of the orphanage." I don't think it explains much. I mean, we're all different, aren't we? Anyway,' she said dismissing her own words, 'I shouldn't be wasting your time telling you all this. We ought to discuss my new chapter. Was it satisfactory?'

14

AS HE AND SUSAN SAT OVER the evening meal he had prepared for them both, a speciality of salmon strips with anchovies, thin-sliced mushroom, and spinach leaf – 'cheap, nourishing, and digestible,' he said self-deprecatingly, to which Susan replied, 'Compliments to the chef', raising her glass to him – Peter began to tell her about his meeting with DeVine. 'Put his tale together with what Patricia Connor had to reveal yesterday,' he said, 'and you've got a first-class mystery on your hands.'

'Fact or fiction?'

'Who knows,' he said, 'you decide. Are you sitting comfortably?'

'Very comfortably,' Susan said. 'No evening rehearsal. Time off for good work.'

'Then I'll begin.' He poured more wine for himself, Susan having put a hand over her glass, and said, 'This goes back twenty years, to when Paddy Connor and DeVine met and became lovers. Well, you know what follows. Paddy discovers she's pregnant, realises she'll have to take a year out and then complete her degree, which she's determined to do, after she's given birth and become a mother. And in the meantime DeVine will find somewhere for them to live – a rented space, from where he can carry on the work of "mitigating" his clients' tax affairs. "Mitigating." That's the term used, I gather, for discovering all possible ways, fair or foul, to bend the rules.'

'Could he do that from here,' Susan interrupted, 'or would they have to be in London?'

'Half-way between. Near enough London for him to get to the office where he still worked, but near enough to the University for Paddy to get to her classes. The University, DeVine reminded me, had just opened a nursery for the benefit of mature students, and for that matter staff members who needed to leave their infants there while they attended lectures and the rest of it.'

'We could have done with that nursery when Paul and Sally were little,' Susan said. 'I loved being with them but still ... '

'You were house-bound, yes, I know.' Peter held up his hands, palms toward her. 'Three years when you couldn't teach, and often couldn't find the time for practice. I do know how difficult it must have been.'

'I doubt that you do,' Susan said with a short, sharp laugh. 'But don't worry, I'm not going to throw a tantrum.' She reached for her water glass, drank deeply, and said, 'Go on with your story.'

'Well,' Peter said, 'this is where it all gets tricky. Paddy insisted that DeVine should go to Hamburg with her when she went to visit her parents, tell them the "good" news. So they took a train, booked in at a cheap hotel, then she went to confront the parents. Naturally said parents were taken aback at her news. Their daughter, brought up to expect only the best, sent to good schools, and all the rest of it, letting herself become pregnant by a man about whom they knew nothing. DeVine, by the way, made a point of emphasising that word when he was telling me about it. *"Nothing."* Meaning not merely someone with no prospects but who was no better than a guttersnipe. Paddy, he said, began to tell them that her lover was already in a good job, someone with prospects, blah, blah, but the father in particular didn't want to know. Refused to shake hands with DeVine, wouldn't even speak to him, but insisted on speaking only to Paddy, referring to her lover as "him", and enquiring of his daughter whether she had any sense of the hurt her parents felt at what she'd done. As if it was all to do with *them*. DeVine told me he could still remember the rage he felt, not so much for himself as for Paddy. She phoned him from her parents' house, both that evening and the following morning, said she needed to spend more time there, wasn't feeling well, and in the end he left for London without her. He had to be back for his work and to tie up a deal with a landlady from whom they – well, he – had rented a small flat – in Wellingborough, I think he said – so he could get to London for work and Paddy could get to the University if and when she needed. Said landlady had accepted a three-month advance which had emptied DeVine's bank account, but Paddy was reasonably optimistic she might be able to get the mother to lend them money to tide them over. He, by the way, was far less hopeful. From all Paddy had told him he guessed the mother might have come round, but the father was the kind of man with ice in his veins and a poker up his arse.'

Peter shook his head as he looked at his wife. 'This was the nineteen-sixties, remember. Swinging for some but for others still a decade of stiff-backed zombies, among whom Paddy Connor's dad could, DeVine reckoned, be considered numero uno.

'And then it got worse. Two days later he got the news – a telephone call from the mother's sister – that Paddy had been rushed to hospital with "pre-natal complications" from which she'd died. But the baby survived. Against the odds, but she did.'

'How terrible,' Susan said. 'How *terrible.*'

After a few moments, she risked asking, 'Was Paddy in poor health, do you know? Might the strain of having to tell her parents about her condition have led to her collapse or whatever happened to her?'

Peter said, 'DeVine reckons the father caused it. Lost his temper, lashed out ... who knows.' And he shrugged. 'It'll never be known.'

'Poor man,' Susan said. 'DeVine, I mean. He must have been shattered.'

'He still is,' Peter told her. 'He could hardly bring himself to talk about it.' He looked at Susan. 'I've always thought of DeVine as a cool, self-contained customer. Not someone you could get close to, or who'd want to let you see what he might be feeling.'

'Like that lad Benjy Hall you told me about?'

'Yes, like him.' But her words startled him, because he was thinking of what he'd been told earlier that afternoon. Mary Hastings' words had come back to him as soon as she'd left his office, carrying with her his usual, genuine congratulations on her work in progress, work which would be completed early in the New Year and due for formal examination, including a viva, in the spring. 'After which I've no doubt you can book your family seats for the July ceremony and award of your PhD. And after *that* we can approach one or two publishers who will, believe me, bite your hand off to get you to sign a formal contract.'

Standing beside the office door, Mary, laughing to hide her pleasure at Peter's words, had said, 'If my hand's been bitten off I'll not be able to sign, will I? Anyway, as my father would always say, never count your ducks before they're hatched.'

'Not chickens?'

'He said that ducks taste better.'

As the door had closed behind her, Peter thought how lucky he was to be supervising Mary Hastings. And then he thought back to what she'd told him about her relationship with her mother. Was there something missing from her account? 'You mustn't think my mother was cold or indifferent.' However you spoke those words they lacked – didn't they? – much sense of deep affection, of what Wordsworth might have called natural warmth. Wordsworth! Himself orphaned as a small boy but, of course, with a sister. 'My dear, dear sister,' he called Dorothy. Some critics had even suggested that their relationship might have been incestuous, like Byron and Augusta's. But Byron's life was a world apart from Wordsworth's. Wordsworth had few close friends, Byron was surrounded by chums and lovers, a social being if also given to moods of black introspection.

Mary Hastings was different again, she had siblings, so she had assured Peter, and he believed her, who were part of an untroubled social group, her mother was kind and loving. DeVine, unlikely any of the others, had nobody. As with that schoolmate of Peter's earlier days, Benjy Hall, DeVine had no parents, no siblings, *nobody*. Until, that is, Paddy gleamed upon his sight, dazzled him. And then the gleam was snuffed out. DeVine was a man alone.

He was hauled back to the present by Susan telling him that Paul had written a brief letter which she'd found waiting on the doormat as soon as she got home from school. 'It was addressed to us both so I felt free to open it.'

'And?'

Susan pushed a scrap of paper over to Peter. 'He says he can't leave for Africa as soon as he'd been hoping. He has to see out his contract in London which has another three months to run, and anyway it takes longer than he'd assumed to tick all the boxes at the Commonwealth Office.'

Peter scanned their son's note and said, half to himself, 'If you ask me, I'd say he's having second thoughts.'

'You think that too?'

Their eyes met and Peter saw the soft gleam of – hope, was it? – in Susan's expression. But she said nothing, was waiting for him to speak. 'He may change his mind again,' he said. 'There's plenty of time before he has to make a final decision.'

They left it at that.

15

THE NEXT DAY, SATURDAY, PETER AND Susan arranged to meet Jim and Clarrie Hobbs for an evening meal at one of the city's new Spanish restaurants. For some years now they had taken it by turn to agree on where they would dine out. Meals at each other's houses, which at an earlier period they had tried, were by tacit agreement no longer mentioned. If the Hobbs came to the Simpsons, Jim, normally the friendliest and most civil of men, became over the course of an evening increasingly drunk and argumentative, on one occasion toppling off his chair and vomiting over a new-laid carpet before he subsided into sleep; and if the Simpsons went to the Hobbs, he was liable to become even drunker. Beside, Clarrie always produced the same meal for every occasion, a beef casserole remarkable for the large quantity of its carrots and the near-invisibility of any meat. Peter was reminded of an old joke about the man at a restaurant who, asked by the waiter how he found his steak, said, 'No problem. I peered under a chip and there it was.' A lovely person, Clarrie, but you wouldn't want to take her Home Cookery course.

Eating out was, by comparison, a relaxed, pleasurable

experience. Of recent years, the city's Chinese and Indian restaurants had been joined by an increasing number of Italian places which, in addition to a variety of acceptable dishes, served good-quality wines – 'No further need to put up with chemical lager,' as Jim said; and shortly afterward, the first Spanish Tapas Bar made its appearance in the city centre. Others followed. Turkish, Vietnamese, Mexican, even a Polish café, known to locals as 'Twenty-Seven Ways to serve Potato'. That did not last long, but the others thrived, and as they did so, the steak-and-chip check-cloth diners began to close their doors.

For this Saturday, Susan had booked a table at the recently established El Torro, and the four of them met there at eight o'clock, Susan arriving straight from rehearsal, and before coming to join the others, arranging with a waiter to have her cello stowed in a cubby-hole behind the cloakroom.

'Good job you don't play the double-bass,' Jim said, as she sat facing him, 'you could have over-stretched the management's resources.'

'I checked when I made the booking,' Susan told him. 'The man I spoke to was decidedly impressed by the fact I was a musician.'

'Speaking of which,' Clarrie said, 'we've already made the usual block booking. Jim's annual treat for the Geography Department, secretaries included.'

'Though I can't say they all look on it as a treat,' Jim said. 'Some of them discover an aged aunt who will, without fail, require their attendance that very evening. Holbrook, for instance. He has more aged aunts than I've had hot dinners.'

He reached for one of the menus their waiter was offering them. 'Still, there are more than enough who enjoy the experience. Promise. Now, what are we going to eat?'

Over the meal that followed – they'd settled for sea-food paella with a white wine that Jim pronounced more than palatable, though he managed to restrict himself to no more than four or five glasses, waiting for the Spanish brandy, Peter guessed – conversation, friendly, relaxed, filled two hours of their evening. Shared reminiscences were the signal for explosions of laughter.

'Remember that sweet white wine everyone used to take to student parties?' Clarrie asked. 'Spanish Graves, it was called, with a long "a", though the youth I was with then reckoned it must have come from the rotted bodies in Madrid cemeteries.'

'And as an alternative,' Susan said, 'there was home-made Punch, otherwise known as "Sandbag". Simply put the plug in the bath or wash basin – having first hooked out any stray socks and stockings – pour in bottles of cider, add some gin and scotch, if available, top it off with apple and orange peel, give a good stir with a lavatory brush, and claim it as the real McCoy.' She looked at Peter. 'Remind me,' she said. 'Where did that term come from?'

'Prohibition times,' Peter said. 'McCoy was a Scotch smuggled across from Canada.'

'Probably manufactured in the back streets of Chicago,' Jim said, 'and less potable than the stuff we drank.'

'Remarkably potable,' Peter said.

'Remarkable, certainly,' Clarrie said.

'And you try telling that to the young today,' Jim said, 'they won't believe you.'

Outside El Torro, at the end of what they all agreed had been one of their most enjoyable Saturday evenings for some time, they parted. Clarrie, who had brought the Hobbs family car, offered the other pair a lift back, but Peter and Susan refused. 'A walk will do us good,' Peter said, and to Susan, 'Carry your bag, Miss?'

She handed over her cello, the two women exchanged kisses, and the men said they'd no doubt meet at the University in the coming days.

As Peter, arm through Susan's, cello hoisted by its strap onto his shoulder, prepared to turn away, Jim asked, 'By the way, have you seen any more of that student of mine. Patricia Connor?'

'Why?'

'Just wondered,' Jim said. 'From all I hear she's already being talked of by her tutors as a rising star.'

'I'm pleased to hear it,' Peter said, 'very pleased. Like mother, like daughter. I'll be able to pass the news onto her father next time I see him.'

For some minutes, as they walked slowly down a city street, its pavement crowded with young, late night revellers, the women short-skirted and in skimpy tops, the men seemingly bare-chested, all of them off to bars and night clubs – dressed down for the occasion, as Susan had once remarked – they found conversation impossible. The raucous hubbub of voices, the screams, the yells, the bellowings, silenced them.

But then they turned up a side-street, hardly more than an alley, where all noise dwindled and the few late evening strollers murmured to each other or walked by in silence. Arms linked, Peter and Susan heard their own footsteps as they picked their way over cobble-stones that would take them up to a minor roundabout from the far side of which they could strike out for the University campus, and from there, back on home territory, saunter down the long-familiar avenue, its ranks of chestnut trees, leafless at this time of year, leading them to the contentments of their house.

Looking up at the night sky, seeing the faint outline of a starry constellation, Peter was about to draw it to Susan's attention when she asked him, 'What did you mean when you told Jim you'd be seeing that man, that DeVine, again?'

And when he made no answer, she added, '"Next time," you said. I thought you'd as good as done with meeting him.'

'I have,' Peter said. 'But he'll be passing through on Monday, on his way back to London from Hull, so we've arranged to have what I assume will be a last meeting then. Well, not a *last*, last meeting, you can't ever rule out coincidence and it's always possible that from time to time we'll bump into each other. "Never say never," as my mother used to say.'

They were passing under a street light and he glanced at Susan's averted face. It was in shadow but he guessed that she was displeased by his awkwardly-phrased words. What was he apologising for?

As though in response to a question he'd not asked, she said, turning to him in the fading glow of the street lamp, 'Is it worth it?'

He pretended to be puzzled by her question.

'Is *what* worth it? Worth *what?*'

Irritated, she said, 'You know what I mean.'

'No,' he said, 'I don't,' and they walked on in silence.

But as soon as they were indoors, she turned to face him. 'This pretence that you're wanting to help him, DeVine, when the truth is you're doing it for *her* sake, for the sake of your beloved sacred-to-my-heart Paddy, Paddy Perfect Pupil.'

Once again he was troubled by the sudden flare of anger in her words, the way she looked at him, that stare with mixed accusation and affront, and, surely, a kind of bewildered pain.

He wanted to comfort her, to reassure her – but for what? What was he to say? That she, Susan, was his one true love, that his lasting sadness for a brilliant student whose life had been so brutally brought to an end was genuine though fading, and that only the daughter's decision to become a student at the university her mother had attended – understandable if not something he himself could possibly have anticipated – had jolted his memories awake back into life, his sadness for that wasted life.

He hardly heard Susan tell him, in an angrily tight voice, that she was off to bed. He was thinking of the words she had spat out – Perfect Pupil. Pupil. The apple of my eye.

When he was small his mother had said that of his sister and him. Words he hadn't then questioned but which, as an adult, he'd recalled when he realised that apple could well be a corruption of pupil, that, anyway, pupil was the black gleaming pip at the eye's centre, and that the Latin 'pupil' was, according to some, named for the reflection in the master's eye of the child he was teaching.

He left the kitchen, went into his study, and pulled down his dictionary. 'Pupil', he read, '**1** orphan, ward, an orphan who is a minor and consequently a ward,' and then, '**2** a person being taught by another.' Paddy hadn't been an orphan, although her lover was, and so was her daughter. And so was Mary Hasting's mother. All coincidence but even so ...

He closed the dictionary, put it back on the shelf. No point in getting tangled in word games. Paddy Connor had been his student, and that was all there was to it. Her attraction for him lay in what? The marriage of true minds? No, but she *was* the kind of student a tutor might come across once in a lifetime or, if he or she was lucky, two or three times at most. People looking in on the close relationship between tutor and tutee, so he told himself, could never understand that what pulled them together wasn't attraction of the flesh but the union of intellectual passion, the mutual understanding that was its own reward.

He remembered now the occasion when Paddy Connor presented him with a tutorial essay on Donne's 'The Awaking', an essay in which she compared the way the poet spoke to his lover with how John Crowe Ransom – and how had she got on to *him?* – chose to address his 'Blue Girls'. How deeply she responded to Donne's wit, his welcoming his lover into his world, how angry she'd been at Crowe Ransom's condescension, his taking for granted the right to tell young women how to behave.

'That's what I can't stand,' she'd told Peter as they discussed her essay. '"Practise your beauty",' she'd quoted. 'Who's *he* to tell them to do any such thing? Critics I've read want to persuade readers of what they say is his "suavity", his "civilised" wit. It's no such thing, is it? It's a man, quite an old man, if you ask me, for all the world like some simpering, bent-kneed roué, who's slavering at the thought of all those women there for his delight.'

He'd laughed in genuine pleasure at her anger, her readiness to speak of the poem in a manner that made plain the intensity of her response, her taking the advice personally, not merely as a collection of words on paper. 'You know,' he told her, 'some critics think that Donne is a bit too keen to lay down the law – man's law – too keen to tell women what they should think, how they should behave.'

'Perhaps,' she said, conceding the point. Then she shook her head. 'But the *way* he writes is so thrilling, isn't it? Those line-endings. "I wonder by my troth what thou and I/Did, til we loved." The way he makes you stress "did" – that's the wonder he's waking to. And so is she, his lover. They're in bed, after spending the night together' – she blushed faintly then said defiantly – 'real lovers.'

'Real lovers.' He hadn't then known about DeVine. Standing in his study, he fancied he could hear Paddy Connor's voice, almost as though she were here, in the room, and so strong was the impression that he turned to face where he imagined her words came from.

The room was in semi-darkness, only his desk lamp was lit, but the study was a place of shadows, of quiet, of emptiness.

'Real lovers.' When he'd learnt that she and DeVine were lovers, the discovery hadn't upset him, had it. Her pregnancy, on the other hand, that *had* shaken him. He didn't want to lose the best student he'd ever known. And lose her to someone he was reasonably certain wouldn't share, wouldn't understand, her grand passion. Whereas he himself ...

He must go to join Susan. He snapped off the desk lamp, went out into the hallway, stood alone in the dark.

In the bedroom he saw that she was already under the bedclothes, apparently asleep. She did not stir as he slipped in beside her, but as he put a tentative hand on her waist, she sighed. He raised himself on an elbow, leant over to kiss her, tasted the salt tears on her cheek.

'Goodnight, my love,' he whispered.

There was no response.

16

SUNDAY MORNING. HIS DAY OF DOMESTICITY. When the children were young and still living at home, Sunday was habitually a day of family togetherness, of walks, or visits to country places, of what they called 'jaunts' into neighbouring counties. They'd set out early, with packets of sandwiches, of vacuum flasks filled with coffee, and bottles of fruit juice. But as childhood became adolescence, Sally and Paul wanted to be off with friends, or they'd take themselves to the Sunday flicks, and what had in earlier years seemed a forever routine was now over and done with; time, the old gypsy man, had borne away what had been the present, and was gone before anyone thought to say goodbye.

Peter was downstairs early, and by the time he was aware of Susan entering the kitchen, he had the coffee ready and was already cracking eggs into the saucepan.

He sensed, without turning, her approach. 'The paper's on the table,' he began to say, and next minute her arms were round his waist and she said, commanded even, 'Give us a kiss, guv.'

Over their scrambled eggs, the mood one of leisurely accord, Susan reminded him that she'd be out until late afternoon – 'final rehearsals, tempers lost, tantrums thrown' – and he announced that as soon as he'd washed up, scanned the Sunday pages and then spent some time on student essays, he would begin to prepare the evening meal – 'hardly what the church ordained for the day of rest but I suppose domestic servants weren't included' – and so ensure that dinner would be on the table for when she returned from her long hours at the coal face.

Susan left the kitchen, returned dressed now in coat and scarf and carrying her cello, gave him a long, lingering kiss, said, 'OK if I take the car?' and when he said 'It'll cost you,' he was promised further kisses and sat in a daze of happiness while he heard the front door close behind her and her footsteps fading along their drive.

'I love you,' he said into the empty air.

* * *

Late in the afternoon, after he'd finished his academic chores, he left his study and went out to the kitchen. There, rewarding himself with a glass of bottled beer, he began to gather the ingredients for their evening meal.

Yes, meal. Not dinner. Dinner was what his parents had called the week-in-week-out Sunday occasions when food was put on the table at one o'clock, and dressed in the formal attire they'd worn to mattins – suit, best dress, blazer, school frock – they ate without enjoyment platesful of gristly roast meat, stringy cabbage, and boiled or roast potatoes, with, to follow, boiled sponge pudding and lumpy custard. After which would follow hours of enforced leisure until it was time to troop back to church for the tedium of Evensong. And finally, to end the day, they would return home once more, this time to a bedtime drink of cocoa or

Ovaltine accompanied by digestive biscuits. This was called supper.

Not long after the newly married Peter and Susan arrived in the city, an older colleague had invited them to supper, and Peter, assuming that they could expect an evening of soft drinks and biscuits, had decided that the two of them should eat before they presented themselves at the colleague's house. Some two hours later they staggered out into the night, having insisted that slight stomach disorders were to account for their inability to polish off the 'supper' that had been placed in front of them: roast chicken together with, as public eating places of the time promised, 'all the trimmings.'

After that, they decided to name meals by the time of day.

But once they became parents, Peter and Susan increasingly came to call the main meal of the day 'dinner', whether early or late in the day, though the term was interchangeable with 'the meal', definite article attached. It was when they all sat down to eat together. It was then that, to his surprise and Susan's pleasure, Peter discovered that shopping for and cooking Sunday meals were genuine pleasures as well as responsible duties. And while he fussed over the consistency of the different sauces he concocted, Susan retired to her own room to practice, or prepare school work for the coming week, or simply read. And, also meanwhile, the children were outside, playing with various friends in the garden, their screams of laughter prompting Peter, as he sliced carrots and potatoes and courgettes, to murmur to himself Blake's Nurse's Song from *Innocence*, which even now, with the children gone, their childhoods transformed into adulthood and its various experiences, he still found coming into his head as he stood at the stove this Sunday afternoon and repeated aloud. 'When the voices of children are heard on the green, And laughing is heard on the hill, My heart is at rest within my breast, And everything else is still.' Not 'laughter' as he'd once rebuked a student who'd misquoted the line, '*laughing*. The actual sound, the activity, *doing* it.'

Again, he repeated the lines to himself, 'When the voices of children are heard on the green, And laughing is heard on the hill,' and as he did so he was aware that his eyes were filling with tears. The laughing lessens, fades to nothing, and the garden is emptied of sound. Innocence becomes experience, the world of darkness, of suffering and death.

No, stop it. Attend to your culinary chores, old man, fool and jester, though white hairs aren't as yet.

* * *

Returning from rehearsal late in the afternoon, Susan called out a greeting as she climbed the stairs, demanding a 'cuppa instanter, if not sooner.'

Excellent. 'Cuppa' meant she was in a good mood. And when, a few minutes later, she came into the kitchen, she made for where he stood at the sink, wrapped her arms round him, and kissed him full and lingeringly on the lips. 'My hero,' she said.

'I take it that practice went well.' And before she could answer, he said, 'You've been at it for most of the day.'

'With an hour off for good behaviour,' she said. 'Drinks and sandwiches, supplied by the management.'

'You know,' Susan now said, as she sat at the table, cradling her tea cup, 'when rehearsals go well you feel more alert, more *alive,* at the close, than you did when you started.'

'And when they go badly?'

'That's when you want to kick the cat.'

'We don't have a cat.'

'You'll do.'

He bent to the oven, checked the meat tray before saying, as he straightened up, 'That must be why I've been feeling so bruised recently.'

He hadn't meant the remark seriously, but now, turning to her, he saw her expression as she looked up at him. Putting down her empty cup and holding her hands up and out to him, she said, 'Sorry. It simply happens.'

Then, abruptly changing the subject, she said, 'How long before dinner's ready? Is there time for a quick shower?'

'You look fresh enough to me,' he said, and, as she stood, 'Twenty minutes OK for you?'

'More than enough,' and in an outrageous parody of a professional seductress, her backward look one of lingering temptation, she almost danced out of the kitchen.

The mood of blithe contentment wrapped itself around them as they ate, their inconsequential talk a way of sustaining what Peter called the not so cool sequestered vale of married love.

Then, toward the meal's end, the phone rang.

Pushing her chair back, Susan stood, went across to the Welsh dresser, and as she settled the receiver at her ear, her voice full of delight, said, almost called out, 'Sally, how lovely to hear your voice.'

But almost at once her expression changed to puzzlement, then exasperation.

'*Really,*' she said. Incredulity? Irritation? 'But he hasn't breathed a word of this to us.'

Exasperation, then. She was looking across at Peter. 'As my mother would have said, he really is the giddy limit.'

She listened to more then said, 'Well, I suppose it's better than disappearing into Africa.'

She was nodding now. Whatever Sally had to say was meeting with her mother's approval. 'Sally, dear, tell your dad about it, he's right here beside me.' And she handed the receiver to Peter.

Peter listened to what his daughter had to say, shaking his head, laughing, then, at length, and after speaking his love, was able to ring off.

As they sat over the coffee she had made while Peter was attending to his daughter's words, Susan said, 'What do you make of this? And why, I ask you, couldn't Paul have told us himself?'

'Perhaps he's taken a vow of silence,' Peter said, winking at her, as relieved as he knew that Susan was.

'But it's not happened yet. And won't before the new year, according to Sally. Anyway, it's Trappist monasteries that invoke silence, surely, not communes.'

'And if the move isn't to be until after Christmas, that gives our beloved son time to come up with several more possibilities regarding what he probably calls life choices.'

Before Susan could answer him, the phone rang again.

'I'll take it this time,' Peter said. 'It's bound to be Paul.'

It was. 'Don't tell me, you're planning to join a commune,' Peter said, beckoning to Susan.

'Hello, Paul,' she said, and as both his parents listened in, they heard Paul say, 'Hi. Mum, I gather you've already heard my news. Sally no doubt. And presumably she'll have told you that there's been a change of plan. I want to come up, talk to you both. Would next weekend be OK?'

'It would be perfect,' Peter said. 'Then you can be here for your mother's Christmas concert. Hear her playing Elgar. Yes, well I'm sure you *were* intending to be present, but this way your presence is guaranteed. Sally and Mark will be here, so we can make it a family weekend. And of course, if you want to bring anyone ... '

He looked at Susan who was nodding agreement. But Paul cut him off.

'I'll be on my own. But I really *do* want to see you both. I'll let you know my time of arrival. I'll be on the chuff-chuff.' And he rang off.

'Well, well,' Susan said, as the two of them went back to their coffee, and for all her expression of modified surprise, Peter could sense her ebullience, her joy, even, at her son's news. She scrutinised his face. 'Do you think he means it?' she asked.

'I hope so,' Peter said.

'So do I. You've no idea how this news – how it lightens the load. I've been worrying about him ever since he told us about going to Africa.'

'Ditto.'

After some moments of silence, during which they sat staring at their empty cups, he said, 'It's so odd, isn't it, this experience of being a parent.' And in answer to her look of sceptical enquiry, he said, 'Yes, I know, cliché of the day, of the year. Of the century. But it *is*.'

'And now you're going to tell me that life is full of surprises.'

'No,' he said, laughing, 'I wasn't, promise.'

'What then?'

'I was thinking of Yeats's claim that writers become greater forces if they are parents. Can you imagine it? Yeats playing wheelbarrow races or joining in ball games. Or Yeats skipping! A photograph of that would be good to have.'

'And you told me once that Dickens was a dreadful tyrant to his poor children. A real life Murdstone.'

Peter smiled ruefully. 'Afraid so,' he said. 'But then the history of creative people is ... '

'Is full of contradictions,' Susan said. She went over, kissed him on the cheek, and said, 'And you, my love, are in grave danger of becoming a bar-room philosopher. And to save you – and me – from that fate I am going to take you up to bed. The washing-up can wait. Come along now.'

He went.

17

PETER WAS RUNNING HOT WATER OVER their breakfast bowls and plates when he became aware of Susan's presence. He turned to her, gave an appreciative whistle, and said, 'Can I carry your bag, Miss?'

His still beautiful wife was dressed in what she called her Monday uniform. Grey pleated skirt, plum-coloured jacket, black, high-neck sweater and the tan boots she claimed were useful for banging out rhythms for pupils who had little or no sense of musical time. Some music teachers, she had once told Peter, used a steel ruler as a device to torture the fingers of the more inept among those whose parents forced them to take piano lessons. 'As if that could do any good. You might as well force tin tacks under their finger nails. You can't *make* kids musically adept.'

And when he'd asked what she hoped to accomplish by her teaching, she'd said, reasonably enough, 'Help those with talent, and teach the rest to be better listeners.'

They'd been in bed at the time, two university students discovering the joys of love and aware that in a further six months they'd be in possession of degrees and forced to think about their futures. But for now time was away and they were here, alone in their little world.

He remembered those words now as he heard her leave the house. Remembered, too, how in the early days of their marriage she'd had a queue of youngsters applying for piano lessons under her tutelage; and though that brought in money they then needed, before he had landed the lectureship, it also meant that the one room of their small flat large enough to accommodate an upright piano – bought on HP – was most evenings occupied by teacher and taught, leaving him to work in what he called his study, though it was not much larger than a broom cupboard and couldn't be heated, which further meant that in winter months he'd have to sit there in his overcoat and scarf, and stuff his ears against piano scales and the seemingly endless repetition of a musical piece he came to know as 'The Fur of Lice.'

The tinkling piano in the next apartment. If only.

But with the birth of their children and their own improved salaries, they'd been able to move to a larger house on the edge of the city. It was a time when for many the purchase of affordable property with what house agents called 'all mod cons' was favoured; older, roomier, draughtier houses, such as the one the Simpsons took, were comparatively cheap, and Susan's music lessons, though they didn't completely end, could now be reduced to one or two a week.

And then, as the children grew older and required more of Susan's time as well as his, the lessons ceased entirely, leaving her able to concentrate her attention on her favourite instrument.

In his study, Peter gathered together the books he'd need for the day's teaching, checked that the afternoon's lecture on Keats was in its folder, shrugged himself into his coat, pulled the front door shut behind him, and set out for the half-hour walk to the University campus.

* * *

Some three hours later, after a morning of tutorials and dictating a couple of references for former students, he strolled across to The Swan. There was no sign of DeVine's car in the car park, but the first person he saw when he entered the saloon bar was DeVine himself. 'Where did you park?' Peter asked as he went across, shaking his head at the invitation to name his poison. 'Better not,' he said, 'I have a full afternoon coming up.'

'You could surely manage one of those alcohol-free beers. England's champion advertises them. Beer and Weetabix. Why not?'

'Botham drink that beer? Have you tasted it?'

'Well, then,' DeVine said, 'A glass of low-alcohol wine, with an ice bucket and bottle of soda water on the side. How's that for an offer you can't refuse? You have to drink *something*. I've sold my jalopy.'

'Really? Why?'

DeVine, with Peter following, loaded their drinks onto a tray and led the way to a table on which, Peter now saw, a hand-written sign announced *RESERVED*.

As he sat, gestured Peter to the chair opposite his own, and handed him his drink, DeVine said, 'I'll hire a get-around for a couple of months, just until the new year.' He sat, gazed expansively around. Lord of the Manor. He was plainly in what another man, *any* other man, would have called high good spirits.

'And then you'll buy a new one?'

'Then I'm off to foreign parts,' DeVine said, as the two of them clinked glasses. He drank half of his pint in one long swallow, replaced his glass on the beer-mat in front of him, adjusted it until he was satisfied that it was positioned exactly as he wanted, after which, raising his eyes to meet Peter's nonplussed look of enquiry, said, 'Sweden.'

'Is that why you were in Hull over the weekend?'

'Got it in one,' DeVine said.

'And now you're going to tell me why.'

'There are timber traders in Hull,' DeVine said, as though speaking to someone in need of simple instruction. 'And the source of their timber is Sweden. Not the only source, because Scandinavia is, as relevant parties no doubt like to say, timber rich.'

Peter said, 'If this is going to take long I'd better have something to eat.' Get on with it, he meant, but DeVine, standing up, said, 'Three-course or cheese cob?'

'Cheese cob.'

DeVine nodded and reached for his glass. 'And I'll have the other half,' he said.

As Peter began to get to his feet, DeVine waved him back into his chair. 'I'm buying.'

Watching him as he stood at the bar placing his orders, Peter thought, 'Whatever's going on here, he's changed. And Sweden? Does he mean that he's going there to do some business or is he suggesting he's staying for longer, plans on living there, even?'

That, it turned out, was precisely what DeVine meant. Returning to his seat, a full glass of beer in front of him, Peter's cheese cob placed before his guest, he said, 'Someone told me that Swedish beer is a very different drink from ours, in dear old England, but I'll no doubt get used to it. A couple of months and I'll have entirely forgotten the difference between mild and bitter. Well, cheers.' He raised his glass and once more drank deeply.

'Now then,' he said, his gaze fixed on Peter's, almost as though he was challenging him not to find what he had to say at the very least a surprise. 'I'm primed and ready to explain.'

Which he proceeded to do.

When he'd finished, Peter, knowing he was required to

find words to respond to DeVine's – revelation, was it? – said, 'So you're pretty certain that what you're going to will be – well, secure.'

DeVine looked at him for some time before replying. When he did, and speaking at first slowly, then more rapidly, he said, 'No idea. But then, as others in my position tend to say, what have I got to lose?'

The expression on his face was difficult to read, but he seemed to be studying Peter through eyes that momentarily glinted with derisive contempt. 'And anyway,' he said, 'who cares?'

He left a pause for Peter to speak, and when he didn't, DeVine repeated, 'Who cares?' but this time in a ruminative undertone. 'Who cares?' he said once more, this time loudly. His mood seemed to be swinging almost violently between extremes.

Embarrassed, awkward, not knowing how to reply, Peter eventually said, 'And you say you've been learning Swedish for some time?'

DeVine leant back in his chair, his look now one of indifference; he shook his head. 'No, I said, "Who cares?"'

And again Peter couldn't answer.

Suddenly, DeVine exploded into laughter. 'Only joking,' he said.

Bewilderment was succeeded by irritation. 'Are you now telling me that you're *not* going to Sweden?'

But still laughing, DeVine shook his head. 'No, no,' he said, 'I'm going right enough. But the truth is I don't give a monkey's whether anyone cares or not. Not that anyone does, I know that, but it doesn't bother me. That Little Orphan Annie act was a con. Me as drama queen. Sorry.'

He didn't look especially contrite, but Peter chose to ignore the performance. Instead, he said, 'Ah, well, perhaps you'll find yourself a Swedish beauty to spend your days and nights with.'

It was a careless, or anyway thoughtless remark, but he was shaken by the look of near rage that suddenly filled the other man's eye. When at length DeVine spoke, his voice now husky with emotion, Peter was so intent in watching his fingers slowly close until the knuckles whitened, so aware of the other man's trembling body, that he barely heard his words.

'Fuck you,' DeVine said. 'There's only one woman in my life.' He breathed in hard. 'I thought you knew that.'

His lips compressed into a thin, tight line. Fascinated, appalled, even, Peter watched them begin to work apart, as though DeVine wanted to say more, but then the mouth shut again, and he stayed silent.

The two of them sat in silence. Peter should, he knew, apologise, but how to find the right words? The silence between them lengthened, deepened, and while it lasted DeVine half turned from Peter and began to look with a kind of calculated indifference at the other occupants of the bar.

Was DeVine going to end this by leaving? Instead, after a few more silent minutes, he sighed. 'OK,' he said, still not looking at Peter, 'forget it.'

In the silence that followed, Peter noticed DeVine's body relax a little, the fingers of his clenched fists begin to unfurl, and, eventually, and to Peter's relief, DeVine spoke.

'I thought you *might* understand, but let's not talk about it, eh.'

'I apologise,' Peter risked saying. 'I spoke without thinking. Forgive me.'

And when the other man nodded, he said, 'Terry, given that we're unlikely to meet up again, answer me two questions, will you?'

'Depends what they are.'

'Do you really believe what Patricia's aunt told you, about the father turning violent, Paddy going into early labour?'

'Meaning that you don't.' DeVine's look was inscrutable.

After a moment, he said, 'To be honest, I've no idea whether he did or not. Nobody can know, can they? And frankly, my dear, I don't give a damn. When I went to see her – see Paddy in the hospital morgue – she was all sheeted up. They pulled the sheet back so I could look at her face but I wouldn't. Couldn't. She was dead. Gone ... '

He stopped, his face now a rictus of pain, and Peter thought, I shouldn't be putting him through this.

When DeVine next spoke, it was as though he wanted to be done with the subject. His words came fast, spooling off his tongue in a harsh monotone. 'The doctor – he spoke English – was there, said it was complications, nothing to be done, there'd be a full report, of course, a tragic accident, but the baby was OK.' He was staring unseeingly at Peter. 'Paddy was dead. That was it. End of story.'

Hesitantly, Peter said, far from certain of his own meaning, 'But there was the baby. Patricia. Your child.'

'I don't want to go into all that,' DeVine said, swatting Peter's words aside. Silence. Then he relented. 'They, Paddy's parents, offered to look after her. Insisted.'

His look challenged Peter. 'What was I supposed to say? What could I do? Bring her back to England with me, and then what? I couldn't care for her on my own, could I? I'd have to hand her over to some sort of carer. But I hadn't any money, not a bean to spare. She'd have to be put into some sort of home. Like father, like daughter.'

He shook his head vehemently. 'No, thanks very much.' He was studying the patch of carpet in front of him. 'Anyway, the two of them would have fought me for possession. Gone to law – and no doubt won. They had all the money.'

He shifted his gaze. He was now looking straight at Peter, wanting him to understand. 'Beside,' he said, as though appealing to him. 'Paddy and I weren't married, weren't even engaged. They'd argue I wasn't a fit person to look after an infant ... blah, blah.'

'What a mess,' Peter said, wishing he could find better, more fitting words.

'And then some.' DeVine shook his head. 'In the end we came to an agreement, courtesy of the lawyer they called in. They'd bring up my daughter, treat her as their own, and I'd be allowed to visit her. "Reasonable access", that was what the lawyer called it. So, yes, an agreement was drawn up, I signed, and that was that. They even accepted that "reasonable access" meant as often as I could get to Germany. Which wasn't very often, of course. *I* had to visit *her*.

'Then they came back to England, but nothing changed. They probably assumed I'd soon enough find myself some other woman, and then they'd be in full charge of my daughter's upbringing. They couldn't bear the sight of me, as they made increasingly clear. Well, I couldn't bear having to be in *their* company. Even if her bloody father had never laid a finger on Paddy, I blamed them for her death, for making her feel she'd wronged them, that she'd wrecked their lives as well as her own. Once they'd got her to themselves, they'd have piled the guilt on her, railed at her for getting pregnant by some worthless toe-rag ... '

DeVine paused. 'But as to whether her father went for her, lashed out at her, caused the damage that killed her, the jury's out, I guess, out forever and won't be back. The aunt loathed him, that's for sure, and no doubt she did her worst to convince the girl, my daughter, there were good reasons for her to hate her grandfather. Happy families, eh? You can't beat 'em.'

As he chewed the last of his cob, Peter considered DeVine's words. When he could speak again, he said, 'How do you know that? Know that the aunt hated him?'

'Because she was the biggest snob of them all, that's why. Reckoned her sister's husband was a jumped-up little shit. She admitted *that* in so many words – about the only time she could bring herself to talk to me. I went round there when Patricia had gone to live at her place, and the old girl – old bitch – let me understand that her ward of court had been unfortunate not only to have me for her father but to have been brought up by "that odious, vulgar man".'

'And that was your daughter's grandfather?'

DeVine nodded without speaking.

Peter thought about it. 'And, if you don't mind my asking, what do you think Pat – Patricia – thought?'

DeVine shrugged. 'No idea,' he said, 'and that's the truth. I don't really know my daughter, any more than she knows me. We've never spoken except to exchange polite nothings. "How are you?" "Well, thank you." I once thought of asking her if she was getting enough to eat, but she'd not have understood the joke. Passing strangers, that's us. Father and daughter. United in love? Some hopes.'

He glanced at his watch. 'I'll have to go soon,' he said, 'I need to get the London train, be back in the Smoke by five o'clock.'

'I'll run you to the station,' Peter began to say, before remembering that Susan had the car.

Fortunately, his offer was waved away. 'I've booked a taxi,' DeVine said. 'It'll be here in twenty minutes.'

He was now, Peter decided, more at his ease, the friction, the hostility that had been in the air between them all but dissolved, gone perhaps with the gradual emptying of the saloon bar.

As though to confirm this, 'What was your other question,' DeVine asked. Leaning back in his chair, relaxed, he said, 'Tell Uncle Terry.'

'This may be an impertinence,' Peter said, 'and if it is, feel free to ignore it.'

DeVine, smiling, waved a hand. 'Be my guest,' he said.

It was a gesture that could be taken for a sign approaching friendly relations. Encouraged, Peter said, 'Your surname. DeVine. It's an unusual one. I've often wondered about it.

Do you have any idea how you came by it? I mean, was it the name of either of your parents?'

DeVine laughed, and this time the sound was doubly reassuring. The two of them had travelled a long way in the hour they'd just spent together.

'Cards on the table, I'm a foundling,' DeVine said, 'not so much an orphan as someone with no known antecedents, as the legal registers say.' He grinned. 'Not even a proper bastard,' he said.

'So who gave you your name?'

Leaning forward now, DeVine looked across the table into Peter's eyes. 'It was pinned to the blanket I was wrapped in,' he said. 'I was left in the porch of a chapel in Billingsgate.'

He cocked an eyebrow. 'How's that for a fishy tale.'

'Ha, ha,' Peter said. Then, 'And was this DeVine of the parish, do you reckon?'

'Shouldn't think so,' DeVine said. 'Anyway, nobody at the orphanage I grew up in could find the name in the census, so they said. Guess what was agreed?'

Peter shook his head. 'No idea.'

'Well, then, hear this,' DeVine said. 'Someone, don't ask me who, reckoned that whoever put me there didn't want to leave their real name pinned to me because if they did they could be traced. Though' – he paused – shrugged his shoulders exaggeratedly – 'though whether anybody would have made much of an effort is, I'd say, highly doubtful. Or as Billingsgate might say, "Not bloody likely." There were more important matters to fret about in nineteen forty-one, like when could London expect the next air-raid, which streets would be flattened, set on fire … '

He looked at Peter. 'When were you born?' he asked.

'Nineteen thirty-five,' Peter said, 'six years before you.'

'And ten years before Paddy. Blimey, you were young when you taught her.'

'I was thirty,' Peter said, 'when first she gleamed upon my

sight.' He glanced at DeVine. 'Sorry, I don't mean to sound flippant.'

'No, that's OK,' DeVine said. 'I reckon she had that effect on most people.' A rueful shrug. 'Anyway, I didn't mean you were still wet behind the ears. She told me you were her favourite teacher.'

'More than I deserved,' Peter said, but DeVine over-rode his words. 'Chances are I was the result of some furtive fuck in the night.'

He paused, said as though by way of apology, 'I'm told there was a lot of that going on at the time, bound to have been. Can't say I blame people, can you? If you didn't know whether you'd be dead in twenty-four hours, well, why not?'

Again he paused. 'Were you in London then?'

'A village near Peterborough,' Peter said, 'we were evacuated there at the beginning of the war. My father was too old for active service. He was forty when war came, and anyway he was a teacher. He had to go with his school. According to my mother it wasn't much fun. Suspicious locals – I'm sure you can guess the kind of thing. If anything goes missing, it has to be one of those kids from London, light-fingered Larries spreading their nits and lice wherever they go. And on top of all that the evacuee kids forever trying to find ways of getting back to their mothers.'

'So not exactly a cushy stroll in the country. How did your father cope with all that?'

'Badly. He dropped dead early in nineteen forty-three. Turned out he had a wonky heart.'

DeVine nodded. 'Sorry,' he said. He gazed past Peter, then said, 'Makes you wonder what's worse. To lose your father when you're a kid or never to have one. One for the Wise Men, that.'

When he spoke again, it was to say, 'Well, I suppose the war passed me by. Sort of. My orphanage was packed off to Cornwall, although most of the time I was too young to know much about it. I can remember once or twice being walked down to the sea, but that must have been right at the end of hostilities, not long before we were put on a train and returned to London. All I know about those years is what I was told later, by a teacher who also told me my name. "Terence DeVine." She wrote it down for me, and someone else, a nurse, I think, sewed a name tab into my shirt and trousers. And I got a birth certificate to keep. All mine,' he said. Pause. 'I had to show it when I got my first job. You know, date of birth, 24th May, 1941, parents unknown, blah, blah.'

He was upset, wanted to wave the matter away.

'What *was* your first employment?' Peter asked, 'as a matter of interest, though if you'd rather not talk about it ... '

But DeVine, now back in control, his eyes clear, looked straight at him. 'Office clerk,' he said. 'Not much but I'm not complaining. I'd been well taught, I'll say that much for the place where I grew up. Reading, writing, arithmetic, a bit of English, some biology. Most of us did well at O-level, and then they found us work or helped us go on to college, technical, agricultural, commercial, armed services – grateful to be serving the nation.'

Peter wanted to ask more about DeVine's school years but, as though keen to deflect him, DeVine, rolling his empty beer glass between the palms of his hands, said, 'Commercial College did well enough for me, helped me become an office clerk – "Duties will include typing brief letters and answering the telephone, neatness and courtesy will at all times be essential" – then a bit later, I got the chance to become a salesman. And the bloke who got me the job told me that I'd do better if I went to Evening Classes, studied basic Accountancy. So I did. And then, even better, I got taken on by an accountancy firm, passed exams, and well,' – he stopped, then, with a dismissive flick of his fingers, said, 'there's bread and cheese upon the shelf.'

'And if I want any more I can find out for myself.'

'Or read my CV,' DeVine said, with a wry smile. 'It's all there, in black and white. Just like my birth certificate.' He laughed, a brief, snappish laugh, and shook his head. 'The only thing it doesn't mention is paid holidays.'

'Oh?'

'There were none,' DeVine said. 'I got paid, no problem there. But I decided against the holidays. Not much point, you see, holidaying on your own at the age of eighteen. Go for walks, look at the sea, buy an ice-cream or candy-floss, take yourself to the flicks. Oh, what fun!'

'But surely you had friends?' Peter wanted to ask him, but before he could do so DeVine, with a shake of the head, glanced at his watch, got abruptly to his feet. 'I'll have to go,' he said, 'the taxi will be outside by now.'

As he stood, he said to Peter, 'What's a man made for, eh?'

'I'll come with you,' Peter said, and together they left the bar and shouldered their way through The Swan's swing doors.

'There it is,' DeVine said, waving at a black cab on the opposite pavement.

Peter walked with him to the waiting vehicle, and waited while DeVine settled with the driver that the cab was indeed for him and would be delivering him at the mainline station.

Peter opened the rear door and as DeVine stooped to enter, said, 'You've still not told me how you think you came by your name.'

Settled now into the cab's back seat, DeVine said, 'Nobody knows. When I was old enough I made some enquiries, even went to the foundlings' set up – Coram's Field. No luck. One of my teachers reckoned my mother might have been some sort of a Christian, most people in the 'forties were, sort of anyway, which is why she left me in a church porch. She'd sinned but I was pure. She probably wanted to call me divine but she didn't know how to spell the word.' He shrugged.

'Believe it if you want.' He pulled the door shut. Leaning from the open window, he said, 'Keep an eye on my daughter, on Patricia, there's a pal.' As he spoke the taxi began to roll.

Standing on the pavement, Peter watched the cab pull away, and raised his hand in salutation. A moment later it had vanished from view.

Walking back to campus, Peter said to himself, 'Pal?' Then, 'Believe it if you want,' and decided that yes, he did want to believe it. 'OK, pal,' he murmured, 'I'll keep an eye on your daughter,' and became aware that a student passing him as he headed for the Arts building was staring curiously in his direction.

18

'BUT WHY CAN'T HE LOOK OUT for her himself?' Susan asked, as they sat over their evening meal. 'He could at least write to her, and surely he can invite her to visit him in Sweden?'

'I doubt that,' Peter said, forking up the last of his pasta. 'Delicious, by the way. I'd almost forgotten you can cook.'

'Ha, bloody ha,' Susan said. 'As soon as the concert's over and done with you'll no doubt want me tied to the kitchen range once more.' And as Peter twirled an imaginary moustache, she added, laughing, 'No, my love, you'll never make the grade as a domestic tyrant.'

She leaned across, patted his cheek. 'Never mind,' she said, 'I like you just the way you are. Now, tell me all about your meeting with DeVine. Why is he off to Sweden? Did he explain?'

'I assume he's been head hunted,' Peter said. 'He's obviously highly thought of in the profession.'

'That's a horrid phrase,' Susan said. '"Head hunted." The cannibalism of the business world.'

'It's common enough,' Peter told her, 'including the academic profession.'

'I'm sure it is.' Susan gave a momentary shudder. 'And I can imagine the smug smiles of those who claim to be the successful hunters. But it doesn't make it any less unpleasant. Men in suits thinking themselves all-important.' And she shuddered again, this time a more pronounced hunching of her shoulders. Self-importance, too. It's everywhere now in the world of education. I was at a meeting of senior staff last week to discuss the school's budgeting, and there was a bit of a set-to between the heads of History and Geography about who had prior claim to some bonus money we were due. An argy-bargy, nothing serious. But then the school bursar took it on himself to butt in. He asked permission to speak and when he was given it looked round at us all and said, "I suggest we bend our collective minds to expedite this issue." I thought at first he was joking and began to laugh, but he stared at me and at a couple of others who'd joined in the laughter. "I fail to see why my advice should be thought amusing," he said.'

'If he speaks like that he *would* fail to see,' Peter said. Then, raising the cafetière, he asked, 'More coffee?'

Susan shook her head. 'But the worst thing is that more than one person at the meeting was quick to nod agreement with him.'

'Not good, I agree,' Peter said, 'in fact, bloody awful.' He drank his coffee. 'But signs of the times, I suppose. Administrators all about us as far as the eye can see.'

'Let's hope your friend DeVine doesn't have to put up with that sort of suit in Stockholm,' Susan said.

'More to the point, let's hope he doesn't turn into one. Uppsala, by the way, that's where he's going,' Peter said, 'and he tells me he's been teaching himself to speak the language.' He'd been going to add that DeVine wasn't his friend, not really, but remembering that 'Pal' with which DeVine had left him, changed his mind. Instead, he said, 'My guess is that he'll be fine, do well. He's sharp as a needle, as my old Ma would have said.'

He emptied his cup, got to his feet. 'He deserves his chance.'

'That's the kind of remark people put at the end of references.'

As they carried their plates over to the sink, Peter said, 'I wouldn't mind writing one for him, I really wouldn't.'

He piled their crockery into the washing-up bowl, squeezed liquid soap over it and, as he ran hot water, told Susan, 'DeVine said something to me as we parted company and the words have been nagging at me all afternoon. He said "What's a man made for, eh?" and I've been chasing that round in my head ever since.'

As she reached past him for a clean plate, teacloth in hand, Susan said, 'Well I have to say the words don't seem very memorable to me. "What's a man made for?" – not exactly "To be or not to be" is it?'

'There you may be wrong,' Peter said. 'After all, in their modest way they're also asking a question about the purpose of existence. *And* without the self-pity that Hamlet's allowing himself to indulge in.'

'Now, now.' Susan poked him in the ribs. 'Spare me the lecture. I'd rather know why DeVine's words have been bothering you.'

'Because,' Peter said, 'they're not his. He was quoting. It only came to me an hour ago, just before you got back from rehearsal. You could have knocked me for a Randall six. Just to be sure, I went into the study and checked up. And there it was. I didn't know whether to be more amazed than abashed. Ashamed, even.'

'And so,' Susan said, 'are you going to tell me or do I have to throw dirty water over you?' And she made to reach for the washing-up bowl.

'Not that, *please,*' Peter said, making pretence to drop to his wife's feet. 'Anything but the washing-up water.'

'*Anything?*'

'OK,' Peter said, 'you win. *Little Dorrit.*'

'Don't you call me names,' Susan said. 'Big Bertha, if you like, but I'll not be Little anything, not for you, not for anyone.'

Peter leant forward and kissed her. '*Little Dorrit*', he said again. 'Pancks. He appears in chapter thirteen. He's one of those characters nobody but Dickens could possibly have invented. A man who spends all his days working for others. And when Clenham – he's the main protagonist of the novel – meets him at a less than posh dinner party, he notices that Pancks seems to be ceaselessly on the go, "at it", so he says, helping the others to food and drink, making notes in a little book to remind him of people he has to see, appointments to be kept. So Clenham asks Pancks straight out, "You lead such a busy life?" and in reply Pancks agrees that he does, and puts a counter question, "What's a man made for?"'

Taking a step back, Susan looked in puzzlement at Peter as she said, 'Surely it could have been coincidence that DeVine used the words?'

'Could have been, but it wasn't,' Peter said. He went across to the kitchen cabinet and, reaching inside, withdrew a brandy glass. Holding it up to Susan he said, 'Fancy a snifter?'

She shook her head but went to her seat and sat there, waiting for Peter to join her.

Peter returned the glass to its shelf. 'No,' he said, 'you're right. No drinking on a Monday. Rule of the house.'

Sitting opposite her, he said, 'I remember that I used to discuss some of Dickens' novels with third year tutorial groups, and *Little Dorrit* was on our list. A great novel, of course, and it led to some of the best group discussions I've ever had.'

'Don't tell me,' Susan said. 'One of the groups included Paddy Connor.'

As Peter nodded, Susan said, 'But that doesn't prove that she got her lover to read the novel.'

'Doesn't prove it, no,' Peter said, 'but I'd bet with borrowed money that she did. She wrote me a superb essay on it, far better than most of the published critics I've come across. Knowing her, she'll have got DeVine to read the novel, *demand* he read it. And why shouldn't he have done so? After all, he had plenty of evenings when he couldn't be with her, stuck in hotel rooms or lodging houses, or alone in his London digs. Time on his hands, her not in his arms, and plenty of incentive.'

'Incentive?' Susan asked. 'You mean he did it to please her.'

'He was besotted with her,' Peter said. 'Still is, although "besotted" is the wrong word. He's not stupefied, and I'm pretty sure you can't call him infatuated. I've been thinking about this, and I've come to realise that his love for Paddy really is a life-long attachment. Commitment, even. It's like Beatrice in *Much Ado about Nothing.* Benedick asks her whether she's in love with him and she says, "Why no, no more than reason." She doesn't mean that she only loves him up to a point, she means it's perfectly reasonable to love him. That's what Paddy meant – means – for DeVine. She was – and she is – his entirely reasonable love.'

He stopped. 'Sorry,' he said, smiling apologetically. 'I know this sounds daft. I admit that I've always thought of DeVine as a pushy sod, muscling in on scenes where he's not wanted, passing himself off as acceptable and not knowing – or caring – that he's getting up people's noses. And, well, he *is* like that. The orphan boy, foundling as I now know – wanting to make good. But Paddy saw what everyone else missed. How intelligent he was and how much he longed to be able to love and be loved. At a guess that changed him forever, transformed him. At all events, I don't think that I've ever come across and – there's no way of not making this sound excessive – I don't think I've ever come across such love. Love lasting. It's as though she's somehow still with him. He'll never be able to, never *want* to let her go.'

And when Susan, unclasping her hands from where they lay resting on her side of the table, seemed about to demur, he told her about that lunchtime's appalling mistake, as he realised it was. 'Suggesting he could find himself a Swedish beauty. I mean Paddy's been dead for twenty years. Not to him, though. I thought for a moment he was going to hit me, or take me by the throat, become really violent. *That's* what I mean when I say I've never known love quite like that.'

But Susan wasn't convinced. 'For all you know, being married to her would have knocked the gloss off the other for both of them. And that, my love, is what Beatrice probably meant. Reasonable love. Loving within reason. Loving in unillusioned knowledge of the other person's blemishes.' She reached across, put a hand against his cheek. 'As I love you for all your faults, your leaving the car with hardly any petrol in it, for example, so I had to get someone to push me the last few yards onto the petrol station forecourt this morning, and as a consequence was late for my first class.'

'Oh, lord, sorry about that,' Peter said, 'I should have remembered. Forgive an old man his errant ways.'

They sat in silence for some minutes.

'But about DeVine.' He was determined, if he could, to make her see. 'Think of that poem of Hardy's,' he said, 'the one you set for last year's school concert.'

'"The Voice?"' Susan's look was one of sceptical enquiry.

'That's it, that's the one. The poem where he talks to his dead wife, tells her that he can still hear her calling to him, that her voice is an inseparable part of the landscape he knows. That though she's now not present she's a presence, she's alive for *him*. "Woman much missed, how you call to me, call to me." You see, she's still real to Hardy, as Paddy Connor is real to DeVine, so real that he can't begin to think of taking another lover.'

His voice was, he knew, beginning to tremble with unexpected emotion, as he said, 'The way he looked at me, I knew that I'd let him down, that he'd begun to think I was a sort of friend, that he could trust me to understand. Instead of which, I'd shown him I didn't care, didn't take him seriously. He called me "Pal" when he went off in the taxi, but "Pal" can be a threatening word, can't it? "You'd better do as I say."'

But Susan shook her head. 'I'd say he was still hoping you might be on friendly terms. And as to Hardy, in the first place he admits that he and his wife weren't happy, and in the second, he re-married, didn't he?'

'And made another woman miserable.' He looked at her. 'Probably because he couldn't let go of his first wife. She went on calling to him.' He sat in thought for a moment, then he said, 'DeVine will never marry.'

'And that's why he's made for work, is that what he meant?'

Susan's words startled him. 'That hadn't occurred to me,' he said, 'but of course you're right. I was thinking he meant that men have no choice but to work. It's the universal condition, the curse of Cain. "In the sweat of thy brow ..." But, yes, what you say makes better sense. It was his way of telling me that since Paddy Connor's death he's no alternative but to fill his life with work, and that my stupid remark about Swedish women showed how little I understood him.'

He was silent for some moments. 'Well,' he said at length, 'at least Sweden will take him away from England. He must know that there's not much prospect of his daughter needing or wanting him around. And if sometime in the future she chooses to get in touch, she'll know where he is. He's bound to let her have his Swedish address, though to be honest I doubt she *will* want to contact him. And he'll think that, too.'

'Why are you so sure?' Susan stood, hands resting on her chair back as she looked enquiringly at her husband.

'Because she almost certainly distrusts him. She'll have grown up believing he was at least partly responsible for her mother's death. And after all he was never around for her. Occasional visits, being watched like a hawk whenever he was with her, and all the time she was having poison dripped in her ear, first by her grandparents and then, when they decamped to Spain, by the great-aunt. She'd have no reason to disbelieve them. He'd be public enemy Number One, so he must have thought, even if it wasn't true, and it very probably was.'

He followed Susan upstairs, and as she pushed open their bedroom door, he said, 'DeVine the foundling. A man without friends or connections.'

Even to himself the words sounded ridiculously melodramatic, and he was relieved when Susan, laughing, said, 'Don't forget the Swedish connections. And then there's you, his English Pal.'

And although he shook his head in sceptical denial of her words, he was glad that she'd spoken them.

19

FROM HIS OFFICE, PETER PHONED JIM Hobbs to ask if he had any further news about Patricia Connor.

'Why?' Jim said. 'Is there anything I should know?'

'Not really,' Peter admitted, 'but her father's leaving England. For the sake of his work,' he added. 'For all I know he's already in Sweden, which is where he's planning to live – for the moment, at least.'

'Presumably she knows?'

'I'd have hoped so, but they're not at all close, so she may be unaware of his movements.'

'Not much of a relationship, is it?'

Peter was about to agree, but all he said was, 'I promised to keep an eye on her while he's out of the country, which for all I know may be a long time ... '

'Keep an eye on a nineteen-year-old student? Good luck with that. Still, seeing it's you, I'll make a few discreet enquiries.'

An hour later he returned the call. 'Nothing much to report,' he said. 'Ms Connor is, I'm told by them as knows, still doing well. Impresses her tutors, hasn't bitten any of them, gets good marks for her written work, and is regular in attendance at class. Unbelievable, if you ask me, especially given some of the idle sods I have to teach. Will that do you?'

'It'll do me very well,' Peter said.

'So you can inform her father that he has no need to worry about his daughter.'

'I could if I had an address for him,' Peter said, 'but thanks, Jim, and remind me to buy you a drink sometime.'

'How about later today?'

Peter laughed. 'No drinking during work hours,' he said. 'And I have to be home promptly to feed Susan before she goes off to evening rehearsal.'

'Oh, yes,' Jim Hobbs said, 'well, they'd better be good. Tell Susan that we've got our tickets and my lady wife is busy fishing moth-balls out of our evening wear.'

'I'll do that,' Peter said, and rang off.

That evening, as he and Susan spooned up bowlsful of a thick vegetable soup that was his own concoction – 'Note the cunning admixture of tinned mungo beans' – Peter repeated his conversation with Jim Hobbs. 'It seems that DeVine's daughter is proving to be one of the stars of her year. I'd like DeVine to hear about her progress but I realise I don't know how to reach him. I don't even know if he's already in Uppsala or still in London. Since letting me know about his change of career, I've heard nothing from him, nothing at all.'

'What about his London home or workplace?'

Peter was nonplussed. 'No, neither. I don't know where he now lives, and these last few years he's been largely working for himself.'

Susan wiped her bowl clean with the last morsels of her crusty roll. 'The Invisible Man,' she said. 'That was good, by the way, but no, I've no time for cheese' – rejecting the board Peter was sliding across to her – 'I have to go. And while I'm gone you can think of ways to discover the whereabouts of Mr DeVine.'

She stood, kissed her husband on top of his head, and said, 'And now for the good news. Sally phoned just as I got back from school. They're all coming for the concert weekend.'

Peter turned as she was about to exit. 'All?'

'Sally, Mark, and Paul. All three.'

And then she was gone.

As he made himself coffee he tried to think of any way he might be able to contact DeVine. Ask the man's daughter whether she had his details? But why bother? DeVine would be in touch sooner or later. 'It's up to you, pal,' he said aloud.

He spent the evening in his study, working his way through a pile of student essays, sometimes raising his head to think about DeVine, DeVine the invisible man, the man whose name was no more than a label pinned to his shawl. Unclaimed. A foundling. Belonging to no one. A free man, you could say. A man of no allegiances.

But then there was Paddy Connor. DeVine would never be free of her. She was his one true commitment. Not the daughter? Perhaps. Yes, perhaps. Why, otherwise, had he wanted Peter to keep an eye open for her while she was at university, the university where her mother had herself been a student? But then he'd not seemed to care much about the girl herself, had he? She wasn't *really* his, he must have decided. Even her name was chosen by her grandparents. The first version had let them down, revealed herself to be pregnant by a man who, even if they didn't know he was a bastard, had no parents, no respectable background. Easy to imagine that in his rage Paddy's father had lashed out at his daughter and inadvertently caused her to go into labour and, even, brought about her death. *Could* it have been like that?

And as he considered that possibility, probability even, Peter began yet again to wonder *why* Paddy, that brilliant student, had chosen to fall in love with someone so entirely different from the world – the society – from which she herself came?

But did choice come into it? An earlier age might have put it down to fate. The inclination of outrageous stars. But he didn't believe that, did he?

He went back to reading student essays and was still at work when he heard the front door open and Susan's shout from the hall.

'I'm at home,' she called to him. 'Come out wherever you are.'

'A moment,' he called back, immeasurably cheered by her tone. 'Then I'm at your service.'

Before he could pack the essays away, his study door opened and in she came, her face, he saw in the window's lit reflection, alive with delight, joy even.

'Good rehearsal?' he asked, and for answer she went to him, threw her arms around his neck, saying as she did so, her voice an outrageous imitation of some Hollywood temptress, 'Fancy a cuppa?'

'Unhand me, madam,' he said, and then could say no more.

20

'MUM,' SALLY SAID, 'YOU WERE TERRIFIC. Mark, tell my mother she was terrific.'

'You were terrific,' Mark said, adding, 'and I mean it.'

'Me too,' Paul said. 'You were terrific.'

'*You* weren't terrific,' Sally said. 'That shaven head is an abomination. Though your dress sense has improved, I'll grant you that.' She slid off her fiancé's lap and going across to her brother felt the lapel of his shiny black jacket. 'Pvc,' she said, 'I knew it. Or is it shellac?'

As she spoke, Peter, a bottle of Champagne in each hand, entered the room where they all sat. Setting the bottles on the table beside the vase of roses, he said, 'Corny, I know, but we're going to toast the musician of the year.'

'Don't give me any,' Susan said, lying back in her armchair, 'I drank two glasses at the party.'

'So did most of us,' Paul said, 'they helped dull the pain of all those bloody speeches.'

He accepted the filled glass his father held out to him. 'The orchestra leader praises the conductor, the conductor praises the orchestra, the soloist is praised and given roses, and so on ad infinitum.'

But he was smiling. 'Still, you deserved it all, dear Mother, I'll say that. Anyway, you don't have to drink to yourself. Bad behaviour, that.'

He raised his glass to Susan, who held up her hand in acknowledgement as they all drank to her.

'Speech?' Peter suggested, and at Susan's 'Not bloody likely,' they all laughed. 'Nevertheless,' he said, leaning over her and kissing her on the lips, 'and joking apart, you were wonderful, my love. You made the cello sing.'

'Elgar's contribution helped,' Susan said. 'Now,' she raised herself to look around at the three guests, 'let's be Obadiah,' and to Mark, who was looking at her in bewilderment, she explained, 'a family joke. Let's be joyful. Let's be happy. I suggest we all drink to that.'

And they did.

But next morning, as the five of them sat round the breakfast table, Susan, waiting until Peter, apron wrapped about him, had cleared away their bowls and plates, said, 'Now, before you set off back to London I want to hear your future plans. Sit up straight, children,' she said in her best school ma'am voice, 'and tell Mother, please. Who's going to start?'

'Me please, teacher,' Paul said, holding up his hand. 'Any chance of another coffee though, to keep my windpipe clear?'

'I'm just brewing a further pot,' Peter said. 'It'll be along any moment.'

'Then I'll begin,' Paul said. 'So,' he paused, looked at them all in turn, then said, 'as you all know, I'm gay. And as I think you also know, I've decided to join a commune. Not that the two are connected. At least, I don't think they are. I've spent the last two years wondering where my future lies and I still don't know. That's why I want to spend some time in a commune, because there I may be able to see, or be helped to see, a way ahead.

He paused, then said, 'Dear Mother and Father, and dear sister, I love you all, but I don't think you can help me choose what I should do with my life any more than you've already done, and that's been a great deal, as I hope you realise. But,' and now his voice had become altogether more serious, the earlier hint of lightness quite gone. 'It's a difficult time to be gay. This bloody illness – the "gay plague" – as right-wing newspapers are now calling it, has already killed several of my friends and will, I know, do for more. And I don't want to be one of them.'

Another pause. 'And then there's Thatcher.' His voice trembling with suppressed rage, he drank some coffee from the cup his father had re-filled. He waited until the trembling which had spread throughout his body was under control, and then said, 'She's gone out of her way to spread her vile, disgusting poison about us. And none of the oily shits around her protest. Baker, Heseltine, Lawson, Parkinson – Parkinson, I ask you, the unctuous bastard who sings "The working class can kiss my arse" – they go along with whatever she says.'

Again he paused. 'To tell the truth and without wanting to be a drama queen – ha – the truth is, I can't stand it. Plenty of us, including some good friends of mine, are determined to fight back. Proud to be Gay. Out on the streets. I think they're terrific but I don't have their courage, I know I don't. So for the while at least I've decided to join a commune. The one I'm going to be a part of is in Cornwall. It's not a closed monastic order, or anything like, and I'm free to come and go as I please. Though of course while I'm there I'll be expected to join in the work and help in any way the commune directs. Dig and hoe and reap and sow.'

'"Put your queer shoulder to the wheel,"' Peter said, and as they all laughed, however uncertainly, Paul looked at his father, and then, after a moment, nodded and smiled. 'I might have known you'd have come across that poem,' he said.

'Not only come across it,' Peter told him. 'I heard Ginsberg read it in London, in the late fifties. And I bought a copy. *Howl and Other Poems.*'

'When you were a student?' Paul asked, momentarily taken aback by his father's revelation.

'I'd just become a lecturer,' Peter said, 'and soon to be married. I wanted Ginsberg to sign it but he was surrounded by admirers and I had to run to get the last train.'

He waved a hand to Paul, 'And now you may continue, my beloved son.'

'I've finished,' Paul said. 'I've told you my plans for the immediate future, and thanks for listening.'

'Immediate?' Susan said. 'When will you be going to Cornwall, then?'

'Next week,' Paul said, 'leaving all my worldly goods to a good cause, of which, believe me, there are plenty, and far more than said goods. I travel light.'

He drank his coffee and, as he replaced the cup in its saucer, grinned at Sally, sighing extravagantly as he did so and wiping imaginary sweat from his brow. 'Over to you, dear sister,' he said.

'There's not much to tell,' Sally said. 'I'm happy with my work, and happy with my life. I feel almost guilty to be saying so but that's how it is. And Mark and I are looking for a flat to share.'

'Oh?'

Sally laughed. 'No, sorry, Mum, we're just good friends. I mean we have no marriage plans if that's what you were hoping. We're fine as we are. Aren't we?' She turned to her lover, who nodded and then said, 'We'd prefer the future to take care of itself.'

He looked at Sally, then round the table. 'Though I've never really understood what that means.'

'Give it time?' Paul suggested. And to Sally he said, 'But keep me informed of any developments, won't you?'

'You're not about to be shut away from the world, then?'

'No chance of that,' Paul told Mark. 'I'll be in regular touch with you all.

'And now,' he said, after a moment's silence and with a wave of his hand to indicate his parents, 'we're waiting to hear your plans.'

And, 'Yes, please,' Sally said.

'We don't have any, do we?' Peter asked Susan, who replied, 'Steady as she goes.'

'Not very exciting, is it?' Paul said to his sister, who said, 'Still, it's good to know there's always somewhere to turn when skies are grey.'

'We're the ones turning grey,' Susan said. She spoke the words lightly enough but she felt a sudden stab of sadness. Looking at the young faces, especially the eager, unmarked faces of her two children, she thought, 'I'm losing them, aren't I. They don't need me any longer.' And as she did so she remembered a remark her own mother had made, not long before her death. It had been a windy autumnal afternoon, when the two of them were returning by car from a visit to lay flowers on her husband's, Sally's father's, grave.

Staring from the passenger window, her mother had murmured words Sally couldn't hear.

'Say again,' she asked.

Apart from the thrum of the engine, there was silence. Then, turning to her daughter but not really speaking to her, her mother said, the words little more than a whisper, 'I'm no use to anyone.'

From the driving seat, Susan glanced across at her mother, the deep-lined skin with uneven blotches of powder, the shakily applied lipstick. 'Oh, Mum,' she said, 'cheer up. Never say die.'

Perhaps her mother hadn't heard. Shocked by the

clumsiness of her own words, their unintended thoughtlessness, Susan certainly hoped so, but as some minutes later she helped the old lady from the car, her mother had said, 'Let's hope ... ' The sentence remained unfinished, but a few days later she was dead.

Now, emerging from her reverie, she realised that Peter was telling his three listeners about DeVine. 'Unlike us stay-at-homes he's off to Sweden, to make a new start.'

Sally, who like her brother knew something about DeVine's history from their father's earlier mentions of his name and the death of Paddy Connor, turned to her lover to explain that DeVine had grown up in an orphanage. 'DeVine was the name pinned to his shawl when he was found in a church porch.'

'How's it spelt?' Mark asked, and when Sally looked enquiringly at her father, Peter spelt the name letter by letter.

'With a capital V? Perhaps it means he's of someone called Vine?'

'I doubt it,' Peter said. 'I mean, that possibility is bound to have occurred to him. I know that he made more than one attempt to find out who his mother might be. He went to the foundling hospital at Coram Fields, where someone directed him to one or two registries that might have been of use, but none of them could help. For all anyone knows to the contrary the poor woman could have been killed in a bombing raid. Thousands were.'

'Still, you could suggest it next time you see him.'

Peter shook his head. 'I doubt that will happen,' he told Paul. 'My guess is that I've seen the last of DeVine. He's no reason to come back here. His daughter won't be in any hurry to see him. She was warned off by an aunt who took her in after her grandparents had retired to sunny Spain, and before that he was hardly ever able to visit her.'

And he told them why that should have been, explaining briefly the circumstances of Patricia's birth, the death through complications of her mother, hurrying over the aunt's claim – probably unfounded – that Paddy's own father might have been the part cause of that death. He ended by saying that the whole shebang, as he called it, was an unholy mess. 'But at least DeVine now has the chance to begin a new life.'

'And forget the past?' Mark suggested.

'He's hardly likely to forget his own daughter,' Peter said. 'I doubt they'll be seeing much if anything of each other, but *he* at least will want to stay in touch, know how she's getting on. Help out if that ever becomes necessary. The aunt can't live for ever.'

'And the grandparents?'

Peter turned to Sally. 'No idea. They did the necessary as they saw it. Rescued her from DeVine's clutches, gave her a home, provided for her education, then handed her over and buggered off to Spain. They're selfish people. I've no doubt Patricia came to realise that soon enough. Selfish and forgettable.'

'Unlike their daughter.'

'Yes,' Peter said to Susan, 'unlike *her.*'

He was thinking of the cold fury he'd seen two days before in DeVine's eyes. 'She's not easily forgotten,' he said.

As he spoke he got to his feet and exited the room, leaving the others to look enquiringly at each other.

He was soon back, this time with a sheaf of papers in his hand. Holding them aloft, he said, 'This is an essay of hers, of Paddy Connor's, one I've kept all these years. It was the last essay she handed in before her death. From time to time I've wondered whether I ought to find a way of getting it into print, but it was written more than twenty years ago and I guess the moment has long passed.'

He riffled through the pages, found the one he was looking for and, looking round the table, said, 'Listen to this. It's from her essay on *Little Dorrit,* which she wrote late in the spring term of her third year, after she and DeVine had met and become lovers. She's talking here about a character called Pancks, someone, she says, Dickens imagines as a kind of human steam engine, full of energy, and she suggests in passing that his name may have come from St Pancras, the station Dickens lived near when his house was at Doughty Street. Then she emphasises that for all his energy and machine-like movements, Pancks *isn't* a machine. He tells Clenham – the novel's central character by the way – that he sees himself as made for work. Not "*to* but *for*" she writes. "I think this is an important difference."'

Peter nodded as he said, as though to himself, 'Good point.'

He paused, looked across at his listeners, then back at the essay in his lap. 'But then she goes on to a more important one. Pancks may be machine-like but even so he's *not* destroyed by his function. "He behaves as a machine, that's what he's *for*; but Clenham realises that despite this, Pancks feels, understands, and commiserates with those he has to do business with."'

Again Peter raised his head, gazed around at his listeners. 'Now,' he said, 'hear this. She says that the only way to account for Pancks is, paradoxically, by calling him unaccountable.'

He held up a finger. 'I'm quoting now. "It is not a word to be found in all dictionaries," she writes, "but I found it in Dr Johnson's. He says that unaccountable means 'inexplicable', and he adds that this is to be understood as 'not to be solved by reason; not reducible to reason'."

Another look around. '"Now let us remember"' – Peter shook his head, laughing delightedly at Paddy Connor's moment of pomposity, before continuing: '"Let us remember that Dr Johnson himself is one of the leading spokesmen for reason and good common sense. Hence, his kicking the stone in the road and thus, to his own satisfaction, refuting Berkeley. Nevertheless, he accepts that there are certain matters, or phenomena, beyond what can be reduced to reason. And this I believe applies to a character like Pancks."'

Peter laid the essay down, raising his hands in a gesture of mute wonder as he did so.

After a moment, he said, 'If that isn't truly remarkable, dear listeners, then never call me Carruthers.'

He was attempting to make light of his own response to his long-dead student's words, but Susan could tell how deeply moved he was by them.

Sally looked across at Paul then at Mark, not knowing what she could or should say.

It was Mark who spoke. 'Would I be wrong to guess that you see this character Pancks as in some way like the man your student was in love with? Sorry,' he added, 'I didn't put that very well.'

But Peter waved the apology away. 'I think you put it quite well enough,' he said, 'and I even think, that in a way I can't quite grasp, DeVine might have thought this himself. Unaccountable,' he added.

Paul said, 'So you *don't* think that love affair could be put down to pure infatuation. You know, posh student falls for a member of the hairy, unwashed community. Mid-sixties, the time of hippiedom, princess and pauper come together.'

'So young and yet so cynical,' Sally said to her brother, and Peter, speaking with surprising emphasis, said, 'You're wrong, Paul, quite wrong.'

'Beside,' Susan added, 'you weren't even a teenager when the sixties came to an end.' She smiled at her son, but not enough to take the edge off her words.

'Still, I understand what Paul's saying.' Sally came to her brother's defence. 'You've often told us, Mum, that we were growing up in the wrong decade. Coal strikes and the three-day week, and the Beatles gone to dust. Make Love, not War. Alright, it's a bit silly as a motto, but I'd rather have that than needing to chant Ban the Bomb. Wouldn't you?' She appealed to Mark.

'Need you ask,' he said. As he spoke, he showed his watch-face to her and she nodded.

'Time we were going,' she said. 'Paul, are you ready?'

A few minutes later they all stood beside Mark's elderly Saab saying their farewells in the chilly, early December weather, the sound of church bells, near and far, calling forlornly above the city's roof tops.

'My other car's a Daimler of course,' Mark said, noting Peter's glance at the numerous scrape marks along the Saab's flanks.

He shook hands with his host, embraced Susan, and stood back as Paul and then Sally enveloped first their father and then, lengthily, their mother, in hugs and kisses.

'Shall we see you at Christmas?' Peter asked as the three crammed themselves into the car.

'We'll let you know, promise,' Sally said, speaking for herself and Mark, while, from the back seat, Paul shook his head. 'I've promised to exchange shovel and hoe for civic duties. Christmas dinner for the homeless. But I'll be in touch, never fear.'

The car began to roll. 'Thanks for everything,' Sally shouted through the open passenger window. 'The concert especially,' and 'Agreed, agreed,' the other two shouted with her; and then the car gathered speed and they were gone.

'What do you reckon then?' Peter asked Susan as, back inside once more, they sat among the breakfast things, while he poured the last dregs of coffee into their two cups.

And in response to her enquiring gaze, he said, 'Are our daughter and her partner booked for a journey into marriage? Or will they choose to go their separate ways?'

'No idea,' Susan said, 'what do you think?'

'I think we should leave it for a couple of years and then consider the question again.'

'And by then Paul will probably have left the commune.' She sighed, 'As he leaves most things,' she added.

'Maybe he's made for a roving life,' Peter said.

They sat in silence for some minutes, musing. Then Peter looked at his wife, as he did so smiling ruefully, or was it quizzically.

'Yes?' she prompted him.

'What's a man made for?' he said.